"We need to get out of here."

"What? No." Elena refused to budge. "We have to find—"

Bear growled low in her chest, the sound echoing off the walls closing in around them.

He took aim at empty space along the corridor, but something was down there. Something that rivaled his human senses.

The power cut out. Bear whimpered from the tail end of their search party. Her fear of the dark would override any command he gave, and without her to protect Elena, he was operating blind. They had to get out of here. This whole plan had been a setup from the beginning. Just like before.

"Damn." Cash grabbed for his flashlight. He hit the power button. "Back up. Head for the door."

Elena's hand fisted around the shoulder of his Kevlar vest. Her gasp reached his ears as a single face emerged in the beam.

"Please. Don't rush out on my account," the man said. "I've been waiting a long time for my wife to come home."

K-9 Security deals with topics that some readers may find difficult.

K-9 SECURITY

Nichole Severn

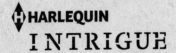

HARLEQUIN
INTRIGUE

To my husband: for managing to keep me from going insane during COVID-19 quarantine so I could write this book.

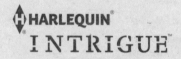

ISBN-13: 978-1-335-59140-1

K-9 Security

Copyright © 2024 by Natascha Jaffa

Recycling programs for this product may not exist in your area.

This is a work of fiction. Names, characters, places and incidents are either the product of the author's imagination or are used fictitiously. Any resemblance to actual persons, living or dead, businesses, companies, events or locales is entirely coincidental.

For questions and comments about the quality of this book, please contact us at CustomerService@Harlequin.com.

Harlequin Enterprises ULC
22 Adelaide St. West, 41st Floor
Toronto, Ontario M5H 4E3, Canada
www.Harlequin.com

Printed in U.S.A.

Nichole Severn writes explosive romantic suspense with strong heroines, heroes who dare challenge them and a hell of a lot of guns. She resides with her very supportive and patient husband, as well as her demon spawn, in Utah. When she's not writing, she's constantly injuring herself running, rock climbing, practicing yoga and snowboarding. She loves hearing from readers through her website, www.nicholesevern.com, and on Facebook at nicholesevern.

Books by Nichole Severn

Harlequin Intrigue

New Mexico Guard Dogs

K-9 Security

Defenders of Battle Mountain

Grave Danger
Dead Giveaway
Dead on Arrival
Presumed Dead
Over Her Dead Body
Dead Again

A Marshal Law Novel

The Fugitive
The Witness
The Prosecutor
The Suspect

Blackhawk Security

Rules in Blackmail
Rules in Rescue
Rules in Deceit
Rules in Defiance
Caught in the Crossfire
The Line of Duty

Visit the Author Profile page at Harlequin.com.

CAST OF CHARACTERS

Cash Meyers—He can spot a threat from a mile away, but he was too late to stop the violent attack on a small New Mexico town. Pulling the only survivor from the debris was supposed to be part of his job as the first line of offense against the *Sangre por Sangre* cartel. But he never expected Elena.

Elena Navarro—The cartel abducted her youngest brother in a massacre of underage recruitment, and she will do whatever it takes to get him back—but she can't do it alone. Relying on the private military contractor intent on keeping his distance, she'll risk it all—including her heart—to stop the cartel lieutenant who doesn't forgive and never forgets.

Bear—The former DEA drug K-9 is more than Cash's asset. She's all that's left of his family.

Jocelyn Carville—Socorro's logistics officer might knit cozy mittens and host movie nights to aid operatives' spirits, but she's possibly the most dangerous asset on the team.

Socorro Security—The Pentagon's war on drugs has pulled the private military contractors of Socorro Security into the fray to dismantle the *Sangre por Sangre* cartel...forcing its operatives to risk their lives and their hearts in the process.

Ivy Bardot—Founder of Socorro Security.

Chapter One

"It's going to be okay." Elena Navarro tried to keep her voice low. It was hard to make sure her brother had heard her over the screams penetrating the windows and doors.

Another burst of gunfire contracted every muscle she owned around Daniel's small frame. She clamped a hand over his mouth to muffle his sobs. They'd hidden beneath their parents' bed, but there was no sign that her mom and dad were ever coming back. "I've got you. I'm not going to let anything happen to you. Okay?"

Daniel nodded, the back of his head pressed against her chest.

Alpine Valley was supposed to be safe. With only two hundred and fifty people in town, the cartel that'd slowly started consuming New Mexico shouldn't have even glanced in their direction. They should've been left alone. Instead, *Sangre por Sangre* had come for blood and recruits.

And Daniel was the prime age to get their attention.

K-9 Security

She had to get him out of here. Had to get him somewhere safe.

"Listen to me. If we stay here, they will take you. I need you to do exactly what I say, and we'll be okay." Elena kept her gaze on the closed bedroom door while backing out from underneath the bed, her hand never leaving her brother's side. Carpet burned against her oversensitive skin, but it was nothing compared to the realization that her parents were most likely dead. "Come on."

He didn't move.

"Daniel, come on. We've got to leave." They didn't have much time. The cartel soldiers would start searching homes to make sure they hadn't left anyone behind. By then, it'd be too late. "Let's go."

"Quiero mama." I want mama. He shook his head. "I don't want to leave."

She didn't have time for this. They didn't have time for this. Elena fisted her brother's shirt and dragged him out from beneath the bed. His protests filled the room, and she struggled to get his flailing punches and kicks under control. He didn't understand. He was too young to know what the cartel would do to him if they got their hands on him. *"Para.* We have to go."

Hiking Daniel onto her hip with one arm, she quieted his cries with her free hand. She hugged him to her, his bare feet nearly dragging against the floor. She wasn't tall in any sense of the word, and Daniel had shot up like a beanstalk over the past years. He was heavy and awkward, but she was all he had left. She'd do whatever it took to get him out of here.

A flashlight beam skimmed over the single window of her parents' bedroom. Elena launched herself against the wall to avoid being seen. The jerking movement dislodged Daniel's black-and-red unicorn dragon, and he cried out for it.

The beam centered on the window.

"Shhh. Shhh." Her breath stalled in her chest. Time distorted, seconds seemed like an eternity and she couldn't seem to keep track of what must have been only an instant. That beam refused to move on. The sound of gunfire had quieted. All she could hear was Daniel's soft cries, but no matter how hard she held on to him, it didn't comfort him.

Shouts pierced through the panes. "I can hear you in there."

The flashlight arced upward. A split second before the window shattered.

Daniel's scream filled her ears.

They didn't have any other choice. They had to run.

Elena hauled him against her chest and pumped her legs as hard as she could. Glass cut through her heel, but she couldn't stop.

"Dragon!" Her brother's sobs intensified as he locked his feet to the small of her back, trying to wiggle free.

"We've got to go!" She ran down the hallway and

headed for the front door. It burst open within feet of her reaching it. A dark outline solidified in the doorway. The soldier's flashlight blinded her, but she kept moving. The back door. She just had to get through the kitchen.

"Where do you think you're going?" Heavy footsteps registered from behind.

Her fingers dug into her brother's soft legs as she raced across old yellow decorative tile. They nearly collided with the sliding glass door. Elena clenched the handle to wrench it open.

It wouldn't move.

Panic infused her every nerve ending. The broomstick. Her parents had always laid a broomstick in the door's track to deter break-ins. The flashlight beam gleamed off the reflective glass behind her.

"Nowhere to go, *señorita*," a low voice said. "And what do we have here? Daniel, right? That must make you Elena. Such a pretty name. Your parents are just outside. Give me the boy, and I will take you to them. Easy."

Easy? No. Her instincts told her every word out of his mouth was a lie. Elena turned to face the shadowed soldier, the light mounted on his gun too bright. She pressed her shoulders into the glass door and crouched. Her thighs burned as she tried to support Daniel's weight. "It's going to be okay," she told him.

"That's right." The shadow moved closer. "You know you can't win. Give me the boy. He'll make a fine soldier."

"Over my dead body." She found the thick broomstick with the broken handle. She swung it into the soldier's shin with everything she had.

His scream punctured through the roaring burst of gunfire. Flashes of light gave her enough direction to grab for the door handle, and she and Daniel fled into the backyard. Echoing shouts and pops of bullets closed in. She hiked Daniel higher up her front, his sobs louder now. They couldn't take her car. The cartel would have already set up roadblocks. Their only choice was the desert. Alone. Without supplies. "We're going to make it. We're going to make it."

She wasn't sure if she'd meant that for Daniel or herself.

"You're going to pay for that!" The soldier who'd cornered them in the kitchen tossed the broomstick onto the back patio. His beam scanned the opposite end of the yard, buying her and Daniel mere seconds.

Elena pried a section of chain-link fence free from the neighbor's cinder block wall. The opening wasn't big enough for both of them. She maneuvered Daniel through. "Go. Run, and don't stop. Don't look back. I'm right behind you."

"Come with me, Lena. Come on. You can fit." Another sob escaped him. He tugged at her hand to drag her through after him.

She shoved at him through the fence while trying to make the opening large enough to fit her, but it wouldn't budge. "Daniel, go!"

The beam centered on her from the back door. Another burst of gunfire caused cinder block dust and chunks to rain down from above. She ducked to protect her head as though her hands could stop a bullet. "Run!"

Her brother ran.

Movement penetrated her peripheral vision. Followed by pain.

A strong hand fisted a chunk of her hair and thrust her face-first into the wall. Lightning struck behind her eyes. Her legs collapsed from beneath her, but the soldier wouldn't let her fall. He pulled her against him. "You've got more fight in you than I expected. I like that. After we find your brother, I'll come back for you."

"No." A wave of dizziness warped his features. She couldn't make out anything distinctive, but his voice… She'd never forget that voice. The ground rushed up to meet her. Rocks sliced into the back of her head and arms. The shadow was moving to climb the fence as she tried to press herself upright. Daniel. He was going after Daniel. "You can't have him."

Her head cleared enough that she shot to her feet. She jumped the soldier as he tossed his weapon over the fence to the other side. She locked her arms around his throat and held on for dear life. She didn't know how to fight. That didn't matter. She'd do anything to stop these men from getting hold of her brother.

"Get off." Those same strong hands that'd rammed her face into the wall grabbed for her T-shirt and ripped her from his back. Air lodged in her chest as she hit the ground. A fist rocketed into the side of her face, and her head snapped back. "When will you people learn? You're not strong enough to fight us." He grabbed her collar and hauled her upper body off the ground, ready to strike again. "We are everywhere. We are everything."

She couldn't stop the wracking cry escaping up her throat as she cradled one side of her face. She spread her hand into the rock-scaping her parents had put in a few years ago. Her fingers brushed the edge of a fist-sized rock. Securing it in her hand, Elena slammed it into the side of his head as hard as she could.

The soldier dropped on top of her. Tears flooded down her face as she tried to get herself under control. She shoved him off, relief and adrenaline fusing into a deadly combination. This wasn't over. The man who'd come after her and Daniel was just one of many. There would be more soon. She had to go. "Daniel."

Elena clawed out from beneath the man's weight and stumbled toward the fence. She managed to squeeze through, but not without the sharp fingers of steel leaving their mark across her neck and chest. Darkness waited on the other side. No sign of movement. No sign of her brother.

She tested the sting at one corner of her mouth with the back of her hand and started jogging. Dead, expansive land stretched out in front of her. Only peppered with Joshua trees, cacti and scrub brush, the desert made it hard to tell where the sky ended and the earth began. And Daniel was out here alone.

"Lena!" His cry forced ice through her veins. Not from ahead as she'd expected. From behind. "Help me! Lena! Let me go!"

Elena turned back to the house. "No. No, no, no—No!"

Brake lights illuminated the sidewalk in front of her parents' house enough for her to get a look at two men forcing her brother into the cargo area of a sleek, black SUV.

"Daniel!" She lunged for the fence she'd just climbed through. Her bare feet slipped in the panic to get back over as fast as possible. She was on the edge of getting to the other side when her body failed her. She fell beside the soldier she'd knocked unconscious. Pain exploded down her arm and into her ribs. It wouldn't stop her.

Daniel's screams died as the cargo lid closed him inside the car.

"No!" This wasn't real. She ran as fast as her body allowed, along the side of the house and toward the front. "Daniel!"

She reached the corner of the house as the car sped away.

The butt of a gun slammed into the side of her head.

And the world went black.

CASH MEYERS GAVE a high-pitched whistle, and his Rottweiler, Bear, launched at the gunman.

Her teeth sank deep into the bastard's arm as the woman the soldier had knocked unconscious hit the ground. A scream echoed through the night, but it was nothing compared to those he'd heard on the way in. Of pain, loss. Of fear. Fires burned out of control from at least three homes that were torched during the recruiting party. *Sangre por Sangre* had raided a small New Mexican town for new blood. And left nothing but devastation.

Bear brought down her target, and Cash called her off with a lower-pitched whistle. His weapon weighed heavy in his hand as he approached the gunman and took aim. "How many others?"

A low laugh was all the answer he received, but Bear's low growl put an end to that. "Too many for you, *mercenario.*" Mercenary.

Cash had been called much worse, but the truth was he and the men and women of Socorro Security were the only ones stopping the cartel from gaining utter control of this area. So he'd take it as a compliment. "It's sweet you're concerned about me, but I've got Bear. Who has your back?"

Nervous energy contorted the soldier's expression in the gleam of flames and moonlight. The man's fingers splayed across the dark steel of his automatic rifle. An upgrade from the last time Cash had a run-in with the cartel. "You'll need more than a dog to protect you if you kill me."

"Oh, I'm not going to kill you." He rammed the butt of his weapon into the soldier's head and knocked him out cold. "You're just not going to be happy when you wake up."

"Steh," he told Bear in German. She huffed confirmation as Cash tossed the soldier's gun out of reach and turned his attention to the woman who'd run head-first into the weapon's stock. Her face came dangerously close to being impaled by one of the cacti, and he maneuvered her chin toward him. Scratches clawed across her neck while swelling and a split lip distorted sharp cheekbones and smooth skin. She'd fought. That much was clear. He set one hand on her shoulder and shook her. "Hey, can you hear me?"

No answer.

Hell, he should've hit the bastard who'd struck her harder. Or let Bear get her pound of flesh. Cash scanned the street. Sirens pierced through the roar of flames and cries. Not even Bear's low whimper compared to the dread pooled at the base of Cash's spine. He'd been too late. He hadn't seen this coming, and now the people in Alpine Valley had paid the price.

Fire and Rescue rolled up to the burning house across the street. One ambulance in tow. It wasn't enough to treat the people gathering for medical attention. Older couples holding their heads, a man calling a woman's name, a toddler screaming in his mother's arms.

Sangre por Sangre had ruined lives tonight.

Because of him.

"Daniel." The woman at his feet cracked her eyes open. Flames reflected in her dark pupils a split second before she slipped back into unconsciousness.

Cash holstered his weapon. She'd taken a nasty hit to the head and then some. She needed medical attention. Now. He slid his hands beneath her thin frame, only then noting that she'd run to the front yard in nothing but a T-shirt and lounge shorts, and hauled her into his chest. *"Aus."*

Bear followed close on his heels like the good companion she'd been trained to be for the Drug Enforcement Agency. With more cartels like *Sangre por Sangre* popping up between the states and butting up against the Mexican border, deploying K-9s like her had become standard protocol, but Bear had taken one too many concussions during her service for the agency. Always the first to respond. Always the last one to leave. She'd dedicated her life to saving lives, and in return, he'd saved her when she'd faced being put down. They had an understanding. A partnership. She was part of the team, and he wasn't ever going to leave her behind.

Cash jogged the way he'd come and wrenched the back door of his SUV open. Bear waited for her turn as he laid the woman in his arms across the seat,

then took position in the front. He hauled himself behind the steering wheel and flipped around as fast
as he dared. Alpine Valley didn't have its own hospital, and the small clinic meant to handle non-life-
threatening injuries would be overrun.

Her groan practically vibrated through him from
the back seat and deep into bone. "Son of a bitch…
lied."

"That seems uncalled for." Cash barely managed
to dodge a police cruiser tearing down the street with
its lights and sirens on high alert. His mind raced
to fill in the blanks that came with her words. She
wasn't conscious. Whatever she'd been through tonight had taken hold and wouldn't let go. It was a defense mechanism. One part of her brain was trying
to process the trauma, while the other tried to force
her into action. "I'm going to get you help. Okay?"

She didn't answer. Out cold.

Putting her in his sights with the rearview mirror,
he couldn't help but catch a glimpse of the devastation behind. It'd take all night for Fire and Rescue
to get the flames under control. Cash hit the first
number on his speed dial on the phone mounted to
the dash. The line only rang once.

"What the hell happened, Meyers?" Jocelyn Carville, Socorro's logistics officer, didn't give him the
chance to answer. "Because from where I'm at on the
top floor, it looks like an entire town has caught fire."

"You're not wrong." Cash floored the accelerator

with another check in the rearview mirror. His back seat companion hadn't moved. "I need additional fire and ambulance units in response from Canon and Ponderosa sent to Alpine Valley. What they have isn't enough. I counted at least three homes on fire and two dozen residents injured. I'm bringing another in."

"Wait. You're bringing who in?" Jocelyn's voice hitched a bit higher.

"Doesn't matter. Can you get me the rigs or not?" he asked.

"I can have them there within thirty minutes." He could practically hear the logistics officer jabbing her finger into the phone. "You owe me."

"I'll have a box of Junior Mints on your desk by morning." Ending the call, he glanced at Bear staring at him from her position in the front seat. "What? I couldn't just leave her there. The clinic is going to be overrun. We have a perfectly good suite at head-quarters. The doc will know how to help." She didn't look too convinced. "Don't give me that look. You would've done the same thing. Protocols be damned."

She cut her attention out the passenger-side window. Her side of the conversation was over.

Cash carved through town. The blaze overtaking Alpine Valley had spread and gave off a glow seen for miles. Every cell in his body urged him to turn around—to do what he could to help—but he had to trust the police knew what they were doing. He turned the SUV onto a one-way dirt road that led up the mountain that overlooked the valley, pinched between two plateaus.

Socorro Security had become the Pentagon's latest instrument in undermining and disbanding *Sangre por Sangre*. Their operation was smaller than most defense companies, but the private military contractors assembled under its banner were the best the United States military had to offer. Forward observers, logistics, combat control, terrorism, homicide—they did it all, and they did it for people like the woman in his back seat. To protect them against the crushing waves of cartels killing and competing for control.

The corner of the massive compound stood out from the dirt-colored mountains surrounding it. Modern, with sleek corners, bulletproof floor-to-ceiling windows, a flat roof that housed their own chopper pad and a black design that had been carved into the side of the range. The one-million-square-foot headquarters housed seven operatives in their own rooms, a fleet of SUVs, a chef's kitchen, an oversize gym, an underground garage, a backup generator, an armory and the best security available on the market. This place had become home after his discharge from the Marine Corps. A place to land after not knowing what to do next—but it was the medical suite Cash needed now.

He dipped the head of the SUV down in the garage with a click of an overhead button and pulled up in front of the elevator doors. He hit the asphalt, Bear jumping free behind him, and rounded to the back seat.

Cash tried not to jar her head more than necessary, hugging her against him. She was still unresponsive, but her delirious name-calling earlier was a good sign she'd pull through. She wasn't talking anymore though, and a sense of urgency simmered in his gut. He wasn't a doctor. While he'd taken a few hits to the head throughout his service, he didn't know anything more than the instinct to get her to a real doctor. He nodded to the elevator door's keypad. *"Tür."*

Bear pressed her front paw to the scanner, and the doors parted.

Once they were inside, a wall of cool air closed in around them as the doors secured into place. His grip automatically tightened on the woman in his arms as the elevator car shot upward. The swelling had reached its peak, but even underneath the bruising and blood, he had a proper glimpse of arched eyebrows, thick eyelashes and a perfect Cupid's bow along her upper lip. He guessed her age somewhere between thirty-two and thirty-six. No hint of silver or gray in a black mane that must've reached her low back. Fit. Someone who took care of herself. Her breathing was even, deep, and accentuated her collarbone across her shoulders. She was beautiful to say the least, but that hadn't stopped the cartel from hurting her.

Bear cocked her head at him, as though sensing he'd taken his eyes off the target. Hell. He hadn't brought her back to headquarters for his own viewing party. She needed immediate help she wasn't going to get back in town.

The elevator pinged, and a world of black expanded before him. The floors, the ceilings, the walls, the art. Monochrome and practical. Cash picked up his pace. He shoved through the door at the end of the hall, swung the woman onto the bed in the middle of the room and got the attention of Socorro's only doctor, seated behind the desk at the far end.

"Hey, Doc." Pointing to Socorro's only visitor, he tried to contain the battle-ready tension in his voice. "I brought you something."

Chapter Two

Come with me, Lena. She couldn't get his voice out of her head. *Come on. You can fit.*

She had fit through the fence, but not fast enough. Her heart threatened to stop beating at the realization. They'd taken her brother, and she hadn't been strong enough to stop them. "Daniel."

"Take it easy." That voice. She didn't know that voice. It was rough and deep, and masculine in a way that rocketed her defenses into overdrive. "Doc said you've earned yourself a mild concussion. It's going to take a few minutes to adjust."

"Where…" Her mouth was caked with dryness and something like dirt. Cold worked through her as the overhead vent pumped out air, and Elena forced her eyes open. Pain arced through her head at the onslaught of lights. "I think I'm going to throw up."

"Wastebasket is on your right," the voice said.

A monitor's rhythm jumped as panic and nausea won out. The garbage can found its way into her hold, and she emptied her stomach with as much grace and decorum as possible. Which wasn't much. It felt good and embarrassing at the same time, but she didn't have the energy to care about either.

"You gotta go slow. Breathe. You've been through a lot, but I give you my word you're safe. The cartel can't find you here." Details bled into focus. A strong nose—broken one too many times—filled a rugged face with a hint of bristle. Dark hair accented even darker eyes, and dirt or ash smeared down his jaw. "Do you remember what happened?"

She didn't know him. And she didn't know this room. The fight instinct that'd failed to keep Daniel safe ripped through her. It centered on a scalpel on a bedside tray and urged her hand to close around the steel. She swung the blade between them and hiked herself higher up the hospital bed. One exit. Through him. She didn't like those odds, but she'd fight. She'd never stop fighting. "Who are you? Where am I?"

A low growl reverberated through the room. Coming from…a dog?

"Platz." One word. That was all it took for the Rottweiler to lick its lips and lie down at the man's command. Mountainous shoulders flexed and receded under a black T-shirt as he scratched behind the dog's ears. "Bear's a drug dog. Former DEA. She's spent years training to sniff out the cartel's dirty little secrets, ain't that right, girl?" His voice softened when he spoke to—what was it?—Bear. Here she was, con-

vinced the cartel had kidnapped her right along with Daniel, and the man beside her bed was baby talking his dog. "She'll follow my every command, but she does not like it when people threaten me."

The scalpel shook in her grip. Elena gauged the distance between her and the door. "I think you have that backward. I'm the one who woke up with no idea who you are, where I'm at or what you want from me."

"Cash," he said.

A ransom request? Confusion took what little strength she had left. The cartel didn't negotiate. Ever. Not with people like her. They took what—who— they wanted and left the scraps of people's lives without second thought. There was no way in hell she'd ever be able to come up with money for her brother. "I don't have any."

A corner of his mouth hitched higher. "It's my name. Cash Meyers. As to where you are, welcome to Socorro Security."

"I don't… I don't know what that is." It was then that she realized the clothes she'd fallen asleep in were gone. In their place was a set of sea-foam green scrubs.

"I found you unconscious at the foot of a cartel soldier. He hit you pretty hard." Cash—if that was his real name—tapped the side of his head to make his point. "I returned the favor, took his weapon and brought you here for medical attention. That understaffed and underfunded clinic you guys rely on wasn't going to give you the care you needed. Figured you're better alive than dead."

She scanned the room. It was crisp, clean and white apart from the casing around a floor-to-ceiling tinted window. The landscape on the other side stretched out around the building, and in the distance, two pillars of smoke funneled upward. Her home was on fire. This wasn't the same clinic she'd gone to in Alpine Valley two months ago. This was calm and clean and white. Not barely hanging on by a thread.

Socorro Security. Judging by the location set into the mountain, this place must've been the military contractor her father had rallied against. Something about aggravating the cartels. Starting a war with towns like theirs caught in the middle. "I shouldn't be here. Take me back. Now."

"It's not safe in Alpine Valley right now, and you're in no condition to go back out there." That hard edge to his voice lost its sharpness, the same as it had when he'd spoken to his dog. "You got a name, or should I make one up?"

Her name? That was his response? The soldier who'd taken Daniel knew her name. How was that possible? Her exhale drained her harder and faster than she thought possible. Elena stretched her feet toward the floor. "I have to go."

Cash stood, blocking her path. "I'm not sure that's

a good idea. Concussion symptoms can strike when you least expect. Take it from Bear."

Take advice from a dog? Yeah. She'd get right on that. She scrambled to collect her clothing from the end of her bed. Bandages she hadn't noticed until now pulled at the tough skin along the bottoms of her feet. She'd run from the house without shoes. It'd be a long and painful trek back to town, but she could do it. She'd get to the police. She'd find a way to fix this. "You don't understand. I can't stay here. My family… They were caught in the middle of the raid. I have to find them."

Her parents must've rushed out of the house to fend off the soldiers. There was no telling what'd happened to them between the fires and the gunshots. Part of her didn't want to know. The other already did know she was the only one left who could get Daniel back.

"Hey." Cash raised calloused palms in surrender. "I'm not asking you to sleep it off and forget about them. I'm saying you're no good to them with potential brain swelling and permanent damage."

She didn't have time for that. Her brother was out there. Alone. Terrified. Possibly hurt. Who else was going to fight to bring him home? Elena clenched her clothing to her chest. She couldn't fight him, just as she hadn't been able to fight off those men, but she'd try. "Please move."

Hesitation smoothed his features into an unreadable mask. "Tell me your name."

He wasn't serious. Of all the things to focus on, he wanted to know her name. But if it was going to get him to move without her having to use force, she'd give in. "Elena. Elena Navarro. Now will you move?"

"That's a start." Cash angled himself to the side to provide a straight shot to the exit. "I'll make you a deal, Elena Navarro. You tell me why *Sangre por Sangre* raided a town of less than three hundred people tonight, and I'll drive you back myself."

"What makes you think I know anything about their motives?" Whatever painkiller they'd given her was starting to wear off, leaving her nerves raw.

A deadliness in his gaze threatened to consume him, as though he was looking for a reason to go back to Alpine Valley and find every single one of those men who'd attacked them. Who'd attacked her. Which didn't make sense. He didn't know her. They were just two specks of dust caught in an unforgiving desert. "Because that soldier who clocked you with the butt of his rifle wasn't going to leave you in that yard. He was about to drag you to his vehicle, and I want to know why. The cartel isn't known for keeping hostages unless they're recruiting, and you're not young enough to cross their radar for trafficking. So what do they want from you?"

Daniel's scream for help echoed through her mind. The pressure in her chest was closing around her throat as memories of his sobs and the feel of his hold around her penetrated the disconnected barrier she'd gotten good at building.

"It's rude to tell someone you just met they're too old to be trafficked." The words escaped her control, and her breath hitched. She'd meant them as a joke, but the truth was right there, wasn't it? Tears burned as seconds distorted in agonizing minutes, but there was no going back. "My brother. He's eight. I think my parents tried to stop the cartel from finding him. I'm not sure what happened to them. I knew *Sangre por Sangre* was going to take him. I tried to get him out of the house, to protect him. We almost made it into the desert, but…" The rest didn't matter. Elena took a step into him. "I need to go back. I know a police officer in town. Deputy McCrae. He can help me—"

"No. He can't, Elena." Something along the lines of pain ticked in the small muscles along his jaw. "I'm sorry. About all of it. It takes a lot of courage to stand up to those men the way you did, but these aren't people committing misdemeanors or getting caught with pot. The cartel is made of soldiers. They aren't ruled by the same laws as you and I are, and they certainly wouldn't think twice about putting anyone down who got in their way. No police force in the country is enough to break through their defenses."

"And you are?" The small amount of hope she'd clung to dissipated. "My father rallied against a group of private military contractors setting up their headquarters so close to our town. He thought having a military presence here would only aggravate the cartels. That we would be caught in the middle of a war. Turns out he was right. So now it's my turn to ask a question, Cash—or whoever the hell you are. Where was Socorro Security when we needed you?"

Physical pain etched deep into his expression.

It created a chain reaction within her that started with wanting to take back her accusation and ended with smoothing those lines from his face. But she'd wasted enough time. And she didn't owe him anything. Elena hugged her clothes to her chest and raised her chin a fraction of an inch. "I'll take that ride now."

"You still haven't answered my question." It was his turn to take a step toward her. "You told me what happened to you and your family, but not why that soldier wanted you specifically."

Shame and guilt and grief combined into a toxic emotional storm. Her name on that soldier's lips grated against everything she was. There was no denying it. Everything that'd happened tonight hadn't been because Socorro Security had failed to do their jobs. It'd happened because of her. "Because his lieutenant ordered him to."

"You're going to need to fill in some blanks here, Elena." Every cell in his body wanted to head back to town and interrogate any soldier he could find, but rushing in without intel or a strategy would only come back on Socorro. Not to mention put Elena in more danger. "Why would a drug cartel lieutenant raid an entire town to get to you?"

"Would you believe me if I told you he's my ex?" Elena released her grip on her dirt-stained clothing and tossed it on the bed. "Of course, I didn't know who he really was until it was too late. I still don't. He used a fake name, told me a bunch of lies to cover up the fact he was working for the very people terrorizing us. Now I'm starting to think raiding Alpine Valley was a cover, and taking Daniel was... punishment."

Cash had had run-ins with the cartel before. Part of the job he'd signed up for, but he'd never wanted to hurt them more than he did right then. Intercepting drug runs, raiding compounds, seizing assets—none of it was good enough. He swallowed the welt of rage clawing up his throat. "Punishment for what?"

"For leaving him," she said. "I don't live with my parents because I don't have ambition or a job or because I don't know how to take care of myself. After we separated, I didn't have any other choice. I had a whole life before I met him. I was a different person before him."

"You were married." The thought shouldn't have bothered him. They weren't friends. Hell, they were barely acquaintances, but the fact rooted deep through muscle and aggravated his insides.

"For a whole three months. That's when I started

seeing the man he kept hidden while we dated. Little things, really. The battery on my phone kept overheating. I took it apart and found some device installed in the back. I think he'd been listening to my calls and following my movements." She picked at her thumbnail, as though trying to distance herself from the conversation, from having to relive what she'd been through. "After that, he moved us to Albuquerque. Wouldn't let me call my parents or make lunch dates with friends. Another time, I thought someone was following me, so I ducked into a shop, and one of his buddies I'd met a few weeks before walked by. After a few weeks, the small things started adding up, but until then I never even realized what was happening."

"He was isolating you." Standard protocol in an abusive relationship. Dominant versus submissive. Weak versus strong. But Cash had no doubt in his mind—based on the defensive marks on her hands and face—that Elena Navarro didn't let anyone have a rule over her. Leaving a relationship such as hers took an unfathomable amount of determination and courage, and, hell, if that wasn't the most admirable thing he'd ever seen. "Did he hurt you?"

Her gaze went distant and sad beneath the swelling around her eye. Elena grabbed her opposite arm, the scrapes and bruising fully exposed to him. "I checked the mail. Something he'd told me not to do when we first got married. Inside there were bills addressed to a name I didn't recognize. Several. To the point I didn't think the mailman had made a mistake. When he left for work the next morning, I had my friend in the police department run the name. Deputy McCrae told me who I'd really married. I don't know how, but he found out."

Tension flooded through him.

"I escaped. I drove to Alpine Valley, and I never went back," she said. "I needed to start over and to be around the people I care about. Now those people are either dead or hurting, and he's not going to stop until I come back."

"Do you want to go back?" He didn't know why the question held as much weight as it did. There was nothing more despicable than a man who mistreated a woman or children, and she'd managed to escape of her own free will. Not all of them did. Cash knew right then and there he would do whatever he could to help her. Help her brother. Help her town.

"Not to him." Her expression broke under a scoff. "But if it comes down to my life or Daniel's, I'll do whatever it takes to protect my brother."

Cash whistled low to wake Bear, who'd apparently gotten tired of waiting around and collapsed on the stuffed bed the doc kept in the corner. He grabbed for his keys. "All right. Then we'll find him."

"What?" Those dark eyes that'd glimmered with fire and deliriousness held him hostage.

"I'm holding up my end of the deal. You told me

why the cartel wants you. I offered a ride back into town in return." He'd already made up his mind and was heading for the door. "We'll start with that."

"Just like that?" Suspicion bled into her voice. "You don't… You don't know me. You said it yourself. The cartel is brutal. They don't live by the same laws as we do. There are thousands of them and two of us. We'd be better off going to the police. Even if they can't help directly, they know people who can."

"Actually, it's more like thousands of them and seven of us. Not including Socorro's K-9s." Bear followed on his heels. The distrust radiating off Elena centered between his shoulder blades as he headed down the hall. He didn't blame her. Everything she'd been through and feeling the physical result of her choices guaranteed trust issues, but she wasn't at fault. The blame was on him. For not seeing the threat before it was too late. For not getting there fast enough. But he'd make this right. "I need to brief my team before we go. Until then you're welcome to crash in my room. Comes with a shower and a king-size bed, and the kitchen is just down the hall. Fully stocked."

"No." A strong hand latched onto his arm and managed to pull him to a stop. "You said you were taking me back into town. I don't want to sleep or shower or eat. There are people counting on me. I have to go back now."

"I know what you're feeling, Elena. I do. You feel

responsible for your family, for what happened to them. You feel like you're the only one who can fix it. But racing back into Alpine Valley is exactly what the cartel is expecting. They took your brother as leverage, to turn you into something pliable and obedient." He couldn't help but pick up on her fear, almost like a solid barrier between them. From their limited interactions, he figured Elena was the kind of woman to stand up to any challenge and stare it down until it broke in front of her, but this wasn't something she could take on herself. No matter how much she wanted it or how strong she thought she was. His arm burned where she splayed her fingers across his skin, and in that moment, it grounded him more than anything else ever had. "If you go back now, half-cocked, without backup or a plan, you'll be walking right into their hands. Is that what you want? Is that what you want for Daniel? Because I guarantee you, even if you do turn yourself over, they won't let him go. They'll keep using him to get you to cooperate, and you'll both be nothing but pawns used against each other."

Her mouth parted on a steady exhale, the force of which brushed the underside of his jaw. She slipped her hand from his arm, and an imagined tendril of cold raced to replace her touch. "No. I don't want that for him. Or me."

"Then let me do the job I was sent here to do." A force he didn't recognize bubbled up inside of him.

Something alive and instinctual. "And I'll give you my word—I will get your brother back."

Elena seemed to steady herself. The pulse at the base of her neck thudded hard against the thin skin there, but at a more even rate. "Why are you doing this? Why risk your life and the lives of your team for someone you just met?"

"Because cartels like *Sangre por Sangre* are like a virus. If they're left unchecked, the infection spreads and kills everything in its path." Especially those radicalized and funded well enough to do some major harm. "My room's just down the hall."

He didn't wait for her to follow. His instincts told him he'd made his point. She wouldn't try to leave on her own. But he could see her walking down this mountain and through the desert to get back home if she put her mind to it.

"You live here?" Her voice had lost some of its gusto. That was the exhaustion kicking in, maybe the concussion, too. She needed a heavy dose of rest. "It's so…"

"Sterile?" That was one way of putting it. Cash motioned her to the third door on the left of this hallway. He automatically angled in after her, noting the scratches across the back and side of her neck as she took in the room. It was weird. Her being in here. This was his space. Well, his and Bear's, and sometimes it ended up being more of the dog's, but it served its purposes. Gave him a place to decompress after an assignment, to recover with his hand in Bear's fur. In here, he wasn't a soldier. Cash was allowed to just…be. "Socorro has to be able to mobilize at the first sign of trouble. We're a security company. We go where we're told and follow orders to a T. No frills. No comforts. If needed, we'll leave this place and set up somewhere new. Although I'll admit I like the view."

Elena didn't answer, seemingly taking in every inch of the room.

From the floating nightstands, to the dark gray walls and wooden headboard of his bed. To the floor-to-ceiling window looking out across the barren landscape. He'd never had any need for something more. Rather, he'd been told what he needed most of his life and accepted it at that.

She closed in on the window and set her hand against the glass as though she could reach out and touch the smoke plumes rising over what was left of Alpine Valley. "You can't fight the desert. All you can do is survive it."

Chapter Three

The smoke plumes had thinned throughout the night.

Fire and Rescue had gotten the blazes under control. Or let them burn themselves out.

Elena sat on the edge of the bed, willing the air to clear hour after hour. Helpless and angry and tired. A headache dulled the vision in her left eye. From staying up all night or the concussion, she didn't know. Maybe a combination of both. Didn't really matter.

She was stuck here until Cash and his team decided what to do with her. He hadn't said as much, but she'd known there wouldn't be any welcome party in her honor. Too much risk to let just anyone walk—or be dragged—through those heavy doors.

But Cash had brought her here.

Which didn't make sense. She could be lying about who she was. She could've made up her entire story, but he'd trusted her. He'd kept her from being abducted by the cartel for no reason other than she'd needed him, and brought her to the one place he considered safe.

But she didn't feel safe.

The cartel would know Cash's face now. They'd know what he'd done, that she was with him, and they'd find a way to get to her. Cash had to know that, too. "They're not going to stop."

The sun broke over the horizon in the east. The sky bled from purple to hints of blue and orange and worked to unravel the knot of anxiety inside. In vain. Cash hadn't come back for a few hours, but his Rottweiler had given up watching Elena with those dark eyes and finally gone to sleep in her cushioned bed.

She couldn't just sit here and do nothing.

Not while her parents were missing, possibly hurt. Not while Daniel was being held hostage. She'd done as Cash had asked. She'd waited until morning and given herself a chance to recover, but she didn't work for Socorro. She didn't have to follow orders.

Elena shoved to her feet. Cash was military. While the cartel only served their own agenda instead of a government's, they considered themselves soldiers. And soldiers liked to hide things. In the final weeks before she'd escaped her husband, she'd found thousands of dollars in cash, keys to apartments, identities she'd never seen before, and communications between him and other lieutenants throughout the organization. And weapons. So many weapons. She hadn't been able to use any of it, but it'd taught her a valuable lesson. Never take anyone at their face value.

Not even a handsome knight in Kevlar.

Bear lifted her head, a low huff of frustration clear.

Elena ran her hands over the back of the bed's headboard, then down into the frame. "If you're just going to rat me out, you might as well help me."

She dropped to her knees and searched beneath the bed. Her stomach growled at the sight of a package of Oreos stuffed up between its frame and the mattress. She unburied it with anticipation. Peanut butter. Her favorite. Wouldn't hurt to get something in her stomach before slipping back into the garage for one of the SUVs. She pulled the package free and sat back on her heels. The ecofriendly wrapping could be heard through the door and down the hall.

Bear shot to her feet in a scamper of anticipation, her back feet nearly sliding out from under her.

Elena hugged the package to her chest. It was almost empty. Probably no more than a couple of cookies left. "If you think I'm going to share with you, you've got another thing coming, Cujo."

The Rottweiler cocked her head to one side with the best plea Elena imagined a dog could give. And it was working.

"Fine. Just one." She peeled back the sticky tab on top of the package. She'd been right. Only two left. Although the frosting didn't look like the peanut butter she was expecting, and the cookies themselves were cracked down the middle. Glancing at Bear,

Elena let the dog take the cookie from her hand as she bit down into hers. "Breakfast of champions."

The bedroom door clicked on steel hinges.

Cash scanned the room a split second before settling that compelling gaze on her and Bear. A hitch at one corner of his mouth released the tension that seemed permanently set into his face. "I see you found the Oreos."

"I was hungry." She tried to ignore the slightly chemical taste swirled throughout the frosting. That wasn't right. These cookies must've expired. Her stomach was ready to revolt as she chewed, but she was so hungry she didn't want to spit it out. "How old are these? They don't taste like peanut butter anymore."

"Couple weeks." His heavy boots thudded over the floor before Cash took a seat on the end of the bed. The mattress dipped with his weight, and it was then that she realized just how...big he was compared to her. Not intimidating. Not forceful. Just mountainous. "I think that's Bear's allergy medicine you're tasting."

"What? No." Elena dropped what was left of the cookie back into the package. The chemical taste coated her tongue and slid down the back of her throat. "Excuse me?"

"Bear's allergic to sagebrush, and she loves Oreos." He was trying not to laugh. She could see it in the slight tick of his eye, and right then she wanted to shove the rest of the Oreo down his throat. "The only way I can get her to take her medicine is by disguising it in a cookie, and from the look of it, she's already got her dose for the day. Thanks for that."

Elena tossed the package across the room and climbed to her feet. She needed water. No. Wait. Alcohol. No. Bleach. She needed bleach to get the taste out of her mouth. It was the only thing that would help. "But you…you hid it under the bed like a late-night snack." Her stomach threatened to revolt. She was going to throw up in front of him. Again.

"Yeah. She'll eat the entire package if I put it somewhere she can get to it." Cash grabbed the remnants of her cookie just as Bear took a step to scoop it up. Tossing it in the garbage, he pulled open one of the cabinets she hadn't gotten around to searching and produced a bottled water. "Good news is, you're not going to have seasonal allergies today."

She twisted off the cap and drank as though she'd been stranded in the middle of the Sahara for three days. It helped. But Elena couldn't help but think the aftertaste would stick around. "And the bad news?"

"You might experience excessive panting and an upset stomach." Cash settled against the built-in desk, massive arms folded across his massive chest. The man would claim the attention of any woman with a pulse with that strong jaw and the promise of reckoning in his body language.

But that smirk was back in place, and she wanted nothing more than to wipe it off by dumping the rest of her water on him. But then what would she use to get rid of the taste of dog medication?

"Ha ha." Elena clutched her water tighter. "I hope you know what you've done. You've officially ruined my love for peanut butter Oreos. Of which I'll mention was an impossible task until now. My mother would be very proud of you."

Her mother. It hit her then, that they'd stepped away from the urgency of the situation and had started talking as though they'd simply met on a day that didn't include a town-wide slaughter of her friends and family. The lightness she'd gotten lost in the past few minutes—the banter and easiness— drained. Leaving her empty.

Cash seemed to realize it, too. The uptick of his mouth was gone.

"You said you had to brief your team on what happened last night." Her mouth dried then. So much for excessive salivating and panting. "So what's the plan? How do we get my brother back?"

"You don't." Two words. That was all he was going to give her? After everything she'd been through?

Her heart threatened to explode straight out of her chest. The fire that'd driven her to fight back against those soldiers simmered beneath her skin. Pain arced through her head. Specks of black shifted in her vision, but she wasn't going to let it stop her from going home. "Then what have you been doing these past few hours? You said you would help me. You said—"

"I gave you my word I and my team would bring him home, and I intend to do just that." He pushed away from the built-in desk as though the conversation was finished. Wrenching open a cabinet door, Cash hit a keypad with a six-digit code. A safe door popped, and he collected a weapon, ammunition and what she thought was a shoulder holster from inside. He discharged the magazine from his pistol and started loading rounds. "I didn't say you'd have any part in it."

Wait. Elena rounded into his peripheral vision, almost stepping on Bear. She got a low growl in response, but the dog's interruption in beauty sleep wasn't high on her priorities right then. "This is my brother. This is my family."

"And how do you expect to help them, Elena? We're trained for this. We're good at this. Each of us has a specialty we've spent years honing. The people in this building—the ones who have my back out there in the field—they're masters of war and are willing to risk their lives for the greater good." He slowed then as though sensing she'd finished his real implication in her head.

Which she had. She wasn't any of those things. She wasn't even close. She was just Elena. She worked remotely for a genealogical website that helped connect people to their ancestry through sending out DNA tests and handing off vials of people's spit. She didn't know the first thing about taking on a cartel, and she knew it. But worse, he knew it. "You're right. I don't know how to shoot a gun or track a target or whatever the hell it is you people do here. I can't protect anyone the way you can."

That simmer under her skin was spreading, growing hotter. To the point it was going to burn her alive unless she did something with it.

"But I was married to a cartel lieutenant. And during that time, I learned a few things about his organization. Things he'd never want to get out."

Cash had slipped back into the soldier again—no more jokes, full-on attention—and she had the feeling being at the center of this man's universe would be a very dangerous place to end up. "Keep talking."

"I saw passports with aliases. I memorized his schedule and the faces of who came around. I documented it all." She stood her ground. Throwing herself in the middle of a war between two opposing military units wouldn't guarantee an ounce of the freedom she'd come home for, but it might get her brother back. She had to try. "And I found keys hidden all over the house attached to little white tags with addresses on them. So whether you like it or not, if your job here is to disassemble *Sangre por Sangre* as you claim, you need me to do it."

Cash didn't move, didn't even seem to breathe, for a series of seconds. Then, life. "In that case, welcome to the team."

HE WAS GOING to regret this.

But they were running out of time.

The longer *Sangre por Sangre* held Daniel hostage, the faster the boy would slip through Socorro's fingers. Cash had seen it done before. The cartel saw kids like Daniel—male and female—as expendable and replaceable as well as psychologically more malleable. Why put years into training a soldier to point and shoot when you could threaten the livelihood and loved ones of a child to get the job done? It was a systematic disassembly of a kid's psyche that relied on protection and guidance. Within a few days, a soldier was born. Not weeks. Not months. Not years.

They couldn't wait. They had to move now.

Awareness added pressure between his shoulder blades as he led Elena across the compound to the conference room, as though he could physically feel her. As though he'd been centered in the crosshairs during that final assignment alongside the DEA a year ago all over again.

Right before his world had imploded. Well, technically exploded.

He automatically reached down for Bear, to hold back the memory, but she'd slowed to walk beside Elena. Traitor. Cash angled to put the two in his sights as he hauled the conference room door open. "Straitjackets are on the right, meds on the left, keep your hands off my crayons."

A crack of a smile softened the tension in her face as she crossed the threshold, and Cash couldn't help but catch her fingers tangled in Bear's fur. Like she'd needed a bit of support, too. Didn't matter how much she tried to convince herself. She was out of her element.

"Ms. Navarro, I'm Ivy Bardot." The founder of Socorro Security—and his boss—rounded the conference table, extending one hand. The redhead with more fire in her eyes than her hair gripped the seam of her blazer. A thousand secrets simmered in the former FBI agent's angled jawline and tight smile lines. Her slim figure beneath her signature slacks and blazers alluded to more investigative skills than strength, but Cash had seen the woman take down more than her share of hostiles without so much as losing her breath. There was an intensity about Ivy that had him clenching every time she turned those emerald-green eyes on him. "Cash has briefed us on your situation. I want you to know Socorro is at your disposal. We will use every resource to retrieve your brother from the cartel."

Elena shook the founder's hand, panic setting in to her upper lip. Her gaze flickered to the rest of the team as though trying to take it all in. The people in this room were operatives, through and through, and unless she'd grown up military, her nerves were going to get the best of her. It made Cash want to close the distance between them, to supply some kind of shield between her and what was coming. "I appreciate that. I don't know what Cash has told you, but I can't... I can't pay you."

"The Pentagon pays us, Ms. Navarro." Ivy backed off, seemingly sensing Elena's tenuous condition. The woman kept her past to herself—as most of the team tended to do—but despite her secrecy, there were some things Socorro's founder couldn't hide. Her intuition, for one. It'd built this place. It'd saved lives. And it'd given him a second chance. "I'm not sure if you're aware, but I met your father a few months ago when the Pentagon announced Socorro would be setting up headquarters here in New Mexico. He ambushed me in the middle of the survey for this site. I was impressed. There aren't many people who surprise me anymore."

Ivy took her position at the head of the conference table and motioned Elena to take a seat down the side, near the door. "He was adamant that we needed to stay away, that our presence here would only make things worse between residents and the cartel. He wanted us to ignore what's happening. Something the men and women in this room aren't willing to do. And I don't think you are either."

Elena pressed her hands into the top of the table,

rocketing Cash's defensive instincts into overdrive. "Then why didn't you do anything last night? If you were sent here to protect us against the cartel, why were they allowed to attack us at all?"

Her fear, her grief, her anger—it all bled into the space between Elena and his team. It stabbed through him and twisted as efficiently as though he'd taken a blade to the gut, and he wanted nothing more in that moment than to take the pain away. But he couldn't. He couldn't take back his mistake.

"I am sorry for what happened on our watch, Ms. Navarro. Truly." Ivy indicated the woman on her right, across from Elena. "Jocelyn Carville—our logistics officer—has recruited Fire and Rescue from the surrounding towns to provide aid, and the DEA is already starting their own investigation into why this happened."

Jocelyn waved from the other side of the table. Her long braid framed her face and brought out the soft undertones of her skin. Of all the operatives contracted to this team, Jocelyn stood as a bright light against the onslaught of violence, darkness and loss any chance she got. Movie nights, hand-knitted gloves and sweaters around Christmas, brownie bake-offs. Cash had never met anyone like her in the military, yet somehow she belonged in this merry band of contractors.

"I've got our combat controller tracking the cartel's

retreat to pinpoint where they're headquartered, and my security operative is checking in with your police department as we speak. Granger here has proven himself as one of the best from the FBI's joint terrorism task force recruited to dismantle some of the country's most dangerous organizations over the past decade," Ivy said.

Granger Morais nodded from the opposite end of the table.

"We're truly doing everything we can to make this right." Socorro's founder had let her attention slide to Cash then back. Ivy knew. She knew it'd been his fault. That an entire town had been burned to the ground last night, that an eight-year-old boy was missing, that the company's contract would fall under review. Because of him. "Cartels like the one who raided Alpine Valley last night claim thousands of lives every year as a result of territory wars, drug addiction and violence. They're linked to political corruption, assassinations and kidnappings, but the *Sangre por Sangre* cartel has somehow clawed its way to the top. They've started killing off the competition and taking more control throughout the state. Socorro is the only thing standing in their way. We have the entire US government supporting us, Ms. Navarro, but we can't do our jobs unless we know what we're up against. You were there last night. You fought them. Is there anything we need to know about before we get ourselves into a war with the cartel?"

"Tell them, Elena." Cash hated putting her in this position, but it was the only way.

All eyes went to Elena. All of this—taking down the cartel, finding her brother, helping a town get back on their feet—it all came down to her. "I was married to one of the cartel's lieutenants. I didn't know who he really was at the time, but I knew he was hiding something. I saw financial statements and mortgage payments to addresses I didn't recognize. I memorized names of my husband's friends and family who came to visit. Though I got the feeling none of them were actually related. So I took photos and made notes of who came to the house and how often."

"For how long?" Granger took note. Always focused, always forceful. Cash didn't normally have a problem with it, but directed at Elena, he had half a mind to tell the terrorism agent to back the hell off.

Elena didn't seem to notice. "Three months."

"Where is this information now?" Ivy signaled for Jocelyn.

Elena's voice—maybe even her determination—wavered. "In my phone. Where I left it."

Hell. She hadn't been carrying one on her last night when he'd dragged her out of there. The cartel had struck without warning close to midnight. She'd most likely been asleep. "Before the raid last night," he said.

"Yes," she said.

They needed that information if they were going to start picking off the scales of the dragon and get Daniel back. But taking Elena back there—where her brother had been abducted, where she'd been about to be abducted—wasn't for the faint of heart. Soldiers trained to live under constant stress and triggers. To be ready to fight at a moment's notice.

"Most phones nowadays have cloud backups," Jocelyn said. "If I get you a laptop, can you access the information remotely?"

"Not this one." The challenge was there. Just waiting to strike. What little he knew of this woman since last night had made one thing clear: she wasn't going to sit on the sidelines while someone else got muddy. She blamed herself for what happened to her brother, and Elena Navarro wasn't going to let anyone else pull that kid out of this mess. But she couldn't do it alone. Not with what he knew about her past and the cartel itself.

"Then we go get it," Cash said. Bear's huff at his feet told him she was all in. She'd had enough downtime. She was rearing for the next assignment. Just like him. It was a trauma response—the need to constantly be on the go, engaged. A distraction from the things really going on in his head. At least, according to the psychiatrist the Corps had forced him to see before his discharge. But in this case, his mental war games just might save Elena's brother. "In and out. We stay under the radar, especially law enforcement. No one even has to know we're there."

"All right." Ivy pressed to her feet, every ounce the leader a bunch of military misfits had relied on when they needed her most. "Cash, you'll lead the recovery of the phone. Jocelyn, I want you with him. Survey the situation and report back once you're clear of the town's borders. Take your K-9 units and stay off the main roads. If there's anything off or the cartel makes a comeback, I want to know about it—"

"With all due respect, Ivy." Cash had never interrupted his boss before, never questioned an order. But this was important. "That's all fine and dandy, but you're leaving out a key part of this operation."

"What's that?" Ivy narrowed her gaze on him.

"The intel we need won't be in Elena's house, and we'll be wasting valuable time we don't have trying to find it on our own." He turned to the woman who'd taken an entire security company hostage with the promise of completing their mission. "There's no way you kept those records on your everyday phone, is there?"

Pure resolve etched into her expression. The slight stiffening of her shoulders was all the answer he needed.

"She hid it. Most likely close enough to town to get to it if she needed it but just out of reach so no one would accidentally come across it." Damn it. Looked as though they didn't have a choice. "Which means she's coming with us."

Chapter Four

There was no way he could've known that.

She'd kept the information she'd gathered about her ex and his organization secret from everyone. Including her family and closest friends. To keep them safe. To compartmentalize what she'd done. Yet Cash had barged into her life and stripped her of any kind of secrecy. As though he'd known her for years. Which was impossible.

Dirt kicked up alongside the SUV as they cut through back roads into Alpine Valley. The smoke was gone, but there was still a burnt smell. From what little she could see through the dust, she caught sight of holes where homes and buildings should've still stood. Nothing but charred ghosts left behind.

Her heart squeezed harder than ever before. She'd done this. She'd brought this evil into their town, into people's homes, into their lives. Alpine Valley had never had a nightlife or a reason for tourists to stay more than a day. Its abundant, nurturing hot springs filled with healing mineral waters had attracted thousands over the years, but it was the men and women she'd known since birth that kept this town alive. Archaeological findings discovered near the dam, the pueblos that were later created, the church dating back to the sixteenth century—these were pieces of her history. Of this town's history. Stories and sites she'd known all her life And the cartel was slowly laying waste to everything in its path. Could all of this have been avoided? Could she have stopped the raid before it'd even started?

The SUV slowed to a stop, and the dirt settled enough for her to see the back fence dividing the desert from the line of her neighbors' homes. Cash and Jocelyn—complete with their K-9 partners in the cargo area—scanned the area like the good soldiers they were supposed to be.

"We'll take a look around." Cash slid one hand behind the passenger headrest and twisted to set those deep brown eyes on her. "Once I give the signal, you can take us to the phone. In and out, remember? No one can know we're here."

She heard Cash's instructions, but they failed to latch on. Because all Elena had attention for was the smoking remains of her childhood home. Air crushed from her chest. "No."

She shouldered out of the vehicle and raced for the hole she'd pried in the back fence to get Daniel out.

The boots and clothing Jocelyn had lent her were a tad too big, holding her back.

"Elena, wait!" Jocelyn's voice pierced through the hard beat of her heart between her ears. A duo of dog barks and the slamming of car doors penetrated her senses, but she couldn't stop.

A rock tripped her up, and she pitched forward. The ground rushed to meet her faster than she expected. It hurt, but the tears were already prickling in her eyes. It was gone. Her home—everything— had been burned to the ground. "No."

Strong hands hauled her into a wall of muscle and turned her away from the scene. Cash buried his hand into the hair at the back of her neck as the sobs took control. "I've got you."

Her instincts had her pushing away to get free, but Cash's tight hold battled to ground her at the same time. It was a war she had no control over. She couldn't breathe, couldn't think. Elena fisted her hands in his vest, needing his support at that moment more than she'd needed anything in her life. The soldier, the one who'd tried to abduct her before Cash interfered, he must've done this. "Why?"

"They're sending you a message." Calluses scraped against the oversensitive skin along her arms as Cash added a couple inches between them. "One you wouldn't be able to ignore. Could your ex know you were gathering intel on the cartel? Did you tell anyone what you'd been doing?"

She finally summoned the ability to release her grip on his vest and wiped her face with the back of her hand. "No. No one knows. I didn't want…" Elena sucked in a lungful of oxygen to regain her balance and risked a glance behind her. The emotional pressure she'd suffered reared its ugly head, and she broke. Right there in front of the man who'd saved her from a fate worse than her nightmares. "I didn't want this to happen."

Too late. Because the tighter she'd held on to that small ounce of power over her ex, the quicker she'd lost it. Until she had nothing left.

"This wasn't your fault, Elena. No matter what that voice in your head is telling you, you are not responsible for this." Cash seemed to hold her tighter then, willing his words to sink in through his touch. It was no use. She knew the truth.

But his willingness to put Socorro's mission on hold long enough to try to comfort her mattered. Seconds distorted into long stretches of breaths as she stared up at him. The early morning sun highlighted the difference between the structure of the bones above his eyes, one slightly lower than the other. She hadn't noticed that before. Hadn't allowed herself to slow down to notice. She wasn't naive. She understood exactly why Cash and Jocelyn and their partners were here. They wanted something she had. She was a pawn, a means to an end. In exchange for her help, they'd help her. A simple arrangement. But it was easy to imagine the past twelve hours hadn't happened when Cash Meyers looked at her as though he was willing to forget his assignment for her. Because there hadn't been a single moment her ex had made the effort once they'd gotten married.

And she should've seen the monster behind the mask long before she'd escaped.

Elena pried her grip from Cash's vest, only then realizing her fingers had gone numb, and took a step back. There'd been moments like this between her and her ex. Where he'd cared. Where he'd comforted her. Where he'd made her feel important and loved with grand gestures. Jewelry, trips, clothing, cars. She'd been blind to who he really was, and she couldn't let herself make that mistake again. "I need to check the house."

She didn't wait for an answer. She wasn't going to let Cash stop her this time. No number of words were going to fix this. The scrapes along her neck tingled as Elena maneuvered through the hole in the fence. She saved herself the injury this time, not in a hurry. As much as she needed to know what was inside, her stomach soured at the idea of finding her parents in the ashes.

Glass and rock crunched under her feet as she approached the mess of smoking wood. She shouldn't have been able to see the street from the backyard. Smoke burned at the back of her throat. The kitchen was almost unrecognizable other than the appliances.

Wood grain cabinets were now scorched with black streaks. The dining table where they'd spent every night as a family for dinner had collapsed. Yellow patterned linoleum had practically melted to the subfloor underneath. There was a diesel smell laced into the smoke.

But no signs of bodies. Then again, she wasn't entirely sure what burned remains were supposed to look like.

"Accelerant. Most likely gasoline." How Cash had fit through that hole in the back fence, she didn't know, but he was there. Helping her search. "Fits the cartel's MO."

She hadn't asked, but once again, he seemed to know exactly what was on her mind. Elena pulled up short of what used to be the living room. "I don't... I don't know what to look for."

"Do you want me to tell you specifics or trust I know what I'm doing?" he asked.

Trust. She didn't have any reason to trust him, and it didn't come as easy for her now as it used to, but she believed him. She couldn't say the words. Instead, she sidestepped to give him access to the living room. "Be my guest."

Bear shoved her nose into the debris and carved a trail down what was left of the hallway on her own. Toward the bedrooms.

Elena was sure her parents had left the house when the gunfire had started, but she'd been so committed to getting Daniel out of the house, she wouldn't have noticed if they'd come back.

"They're not in here," Cash said.

"How do you know?" In truth, she didn't want to know, but despite what little she'd learned about the Socorro operative, she couldn't discount the fact he might lie to keep her on task. Recovering her phone. "Doesn't gasoline make fire burn hotter?"

"It does. Up to twenty-five-hundred degrees, but even then, it's not hot enough to get rid of a body entirely." He marched through the room that'd housed so many memories over the years. Christmases with the tree by the window. Movie nights on the floor and a bowl of popcorn. Her *abuela*'s home-cooked meals around the too-big coffee table. "Human remains assume a distorted position referred to as the 'pugilistic attitude' when the muscles contract due to heat, making them easy to spot. There's nothing in this room other than furniture."

Bear returned, continuing her search through the rubble with something in her mouth. A stuffed animal. Elena couldn't be sure, but she could almost see the tail of a dragon between the dog's teeth. Daniel's dragon.

"Then they made it out." A spark of hope doused the surge that'd held her hostage all night. Her parents might've survived. "Maybe they fled to one of the neighbors' houses or the police. They need to know what happened to Daniel."

She headed for the front of the house where Jocelyn and her German shepherd—Maverick—surveyed the street.

But was blocked by the very man who'd saved her life last night. She backed up, remembering the scorch of his skin against hers. Hotter than the timbers around her. "What are you doing?"

"They can't know you're here, Elena. No one can know. It's too dangerous." Pure determination settled into the fine lines around his eyes, and in that moment, he wasn't the rescuer who'd teased her for eating dog allergy medicine. He was a security operative. A soldier. "We came back here to collect the intel you've put together on the cartel. Nothing more. And the longer we're here, the higher chances someone reports your movements."

Wait. "You can't be saying what I think you're saying." Her nerves were getting the best of her. It made sense her ex would know where she'd run— and maybe she'd been foolish to come back to Alpine Valley in the first place—but to allude that the cartel had been tracking her through the very neighbors and friends she'd known her whole life? No. "You think there are people in this town who are some kind of spies for *Sangre por Sangre*? That they're keeping tabs on me? They're not, and you're wrong."

He had to be. Because if he wasn't… She couldn't think about that. She couldn't imagine any of these people being okay with what the cartel had done.

Elena shoved past him and through the opening where her front door had once stood. It was a fifteen-minute walk to where she'd hidden the phone. And the sooner she had it, the sooner Daniel could come home.

Cash's words barely reached her as she added distance between them. "I hope that's true."

It was always the ones you least expected.

Cash had learned that lesson the hard way. Right as an entire DEA raid had blown up in his and Bear's faces.

Smoke clung to his gear as he left what remained of Elena's house behind. Jocelyn's attention drilled through him. She wanted to say something—most likely encourage him to be more human and not a robot, as she liked to say—but thankfully decided against it as they kept up with Elena.

Part of him wanted her to be right. To believe that this small town had just gotten caught off guard by the cartel. Not that they had anything to do with targeting Elena's brother and home. But Cash hadn't trusted that part of himself for a long time. He couldn't.

Bear brushed against his pant leg as though the same thoughts were running through her head.

He scanned the street. Three more houses had been burned to the ground, but the sound of sirens had died. No faces in front yards. No vehicles driving by. The town had come to a standstill. Residents had locked themselves behind closed doors and had no intention of leaving.

"Have you seen anything like this?" Jocelyn's hand hovered over the sidearm at her hip. The dark gray trousers and white button-down shirt did nothing to hide her weapon, and it only added to what Cash knew about her. Everything out in the open. Ask the logistics officer a question and she answered. No issue. It was one of the things he liked about her best. What made them a good team. "This place is a ghost town."

"Once." He'd trusted the wrong person and nearly ended up in the ground because of it. His gaze slid to Elena a few feet ahead. They moved into backyards as they worked their way down the street. Despite being surrounded by miles of desert, Alpine Valley provided life to an entire natural preserve. Trees over a hundred feet tall crowded in around them, branches clawing at his shoulder holster, neck and vest. It was amazing, really. An oasis in the middle of scorched earth. "Fire and Rescue must've caught the flames before they jumped to the trees."

"Lucky." Jocelyn clicked her tongue to call Maverick back to her side. The German shepherd did as he was told, then jogged ahead with Bear. The woman scanned the surrounding trees. No matter what threat came their way, Cash trusted Jocelyn would have his back. That was one of the things that set Socorro apart from the military. In the marines, he was ex-

pected to serve until his countdown to discharge ran
out. With Socorro, every single one of them made
the choice to stay. Out of loyalty to the team. "What
do you think about her?" Jocelyn nodded to Elena
up ahead.

His mind instantly went to the moment Elena had
fit against his chest. He hadn't planned on pulling
her into his arms, but watching her hit the dirt and
try to claw her way toward her house had broken
something inside of him. It'd been instinct—a connection between them he didn't quite understand and
wasn't sure he wanted to. In less than thirteen hours,
she'd taken hold of something inside of him. Raised
a protective tendency he'd solely reserved for those
he trusted. As much as he wanted to believe she
hadn't known what she was getting into when she'd
married a *Sangre por Sangre* lieutenant, there was
something about her that triggered his defenses. And
reminded him of the masks people wore. "She's in
over her head."

Jocelyn didn't respond to that, which he took as
confirmation of his theory. She was here on orders.
Simple as that. And she didn't intend to fail.

"It's just up here." Muscle flexed through the back
of Elena's borrowed jeans, and Cash's gut tightened.
Jocelyn could've at least given her something un-
flattering to wear on their trek through the desert.

Temperatures spiked as trees thinned. Sagebrush,
muted dirt and exposed terrain replaced lush foliage

and shade. They caught a dirt trail hiking higher into Alpine Valley's historic site. Sweat built around his collar as he took in the outline of the mission ahead. The oldest mission in the entire United States had served as Elena's secret keeper. But like the town itself, there was no one in sight. Perfect location for an ambush. "Jocelyn, take Maverick around the backside. I don't want any surprises."

"You got it." Jocelyn's low whistle drew her shepherd to her side. Both jogged along the tree line, out of sight within a few minutes.

Cash positioned his earpiece. "You read me?"

Elena watched him, squinting due to the sun, as though memorizing his every move. The hair on the back of his neck stood on end the longer they remained out in the open, but the trees were their best chance at cover if this went sideways. Better to cover all their bases.

"Loud and clear," Jocelyn said in his ear.

"Good." He scanned unfamiliar terrain, taking in the ridges surrounding the mission. It was basic warfare. Attack from high ground, gain the upper hand. Like the cartel, the only help from above he trusted was the kind that came with a sniper rifle. "Watch your back."

"What? You worried about me or something?" The connection quieted, giving Cash enough room to focus on the task at hand.

"Where we headed?" he asked.

"Inside." Elena didn't make a move to walk up the incline. "I know why you're here, Cash. I know how important that intel is to you and Socorro. I hardly believe you'll risk your life for someone you just met, but I need to know you won't back out on your word to bring my brother home."

She was persistent. He'd give her that much. And careful. Hell, the truth was he couldn't blame her for either after everything she'd been through. To learn the one person you trusted the most wasn't at all what they'd advertised. He'd been there. He'd lived through the betrayal, the heartache, the anger. And it'd taken him over a year to come to terms with the consequences. There'd only been one bright light that'd come out of it. His dog. "What makes you think I wouldn't risk my life for someone I just met?"

Seemed she didn't have an answer for that one.

Cash started up the incline. The sun beat down on him, but it was nothing compared to the heat generated every time he found himself this close to Elena. It didn't make sense. He'd helped dozens of Socorro clients over the years. Some in more complicated situations than hers. He'd never felt this…connected to any of them. She was different. He didn't know how yet, but the guilt suffocating him from the inside urged him to find out why.

They reached the entrance together. The early sixteenth-century mission pueblo was associated with both Native American and Spanish colonial his-

tory and had played an integral part in the heritage
of the country as a whole. This was sacred ground
in many respects, but organizations like *Sangre por
Sangre* would only see it as a way to punish the people who dared to rise up against them.

Cash's survival instincts rocketed as the stone
walls rose on either side of them. He'd studied the
area when he'd taken the contract from Socorro until
the very elevation changes had been etched into his
brain. But he'd never come here. Too many corners
with a possibility of an ambush. Too much unknown.
Bear could only sense so much with permanent brain
damage. Even on her worse days, she excelled by
leaps and bounds ahead of him, but someday that
wouldn't be enough.

Elena brushed her fingertips against the stone
walls as she walked. Her lips moved without making
sound, as though she were counting the bricks beneath her touch. She stopped suddenly and dropped
into a crouch. "I need your knife."

"How do you know I'm carrying a knife?" He
pulled his military blade from the inside of his right
ankle and handed it off, grip-first. Any number of
scenarios in which she turned that knife on him and
made a run for it crossed his mind. He'd gone and put
himself in a position he'd sworn never to again. He'd
gotten personally involved in seeing this through.

"Soldiers always come prepared." Scabbed skin
brushed against the tops of his fingers and sent an

electric bolt of awareness down his spine. It was unlike anything he'd experienced, yet he couldn't say the same for Elena. She wedged the tip of his knife into the space between two stones and tried to pry one free. As though the reaction between them had never happened. Maybe it hadn't. "Army?"

"Marine Corps. Twenty years." The wind kicked up, cascading dust around her in a translucent veil of glitter. It enriched the color of her eyes and stood out in specks in her hair. Like she'd been touched by something otherworldly.

"And you thought two decades wasn't near long enough to take orders from people who aren't in the mess with you?" Elena handed him the knife and gripped both sides of the stone she'd worked free. Tugging it lose, she set it beside her and crouched to get a better look inside.

He didn't have any reason to answer her question. In fact, he didn't owe her anything, but Cash couldn't fight his need to explain. "I was discharged after a joint assignment between the DEA and the Corps went sideways. I'd been tracking a cartel coming up out of Colombia. Thought I knew everything I needed to know."

Elena pulled a stained dishrag from the hole she'd made in the wall, staring up at him. "What happened?"

"Didn't so much as get a foot in the compound before we were made." His grip went to the butt of his sidearm. "Bullets started flying, and at the time, I just kept asking myself where the hell I went wrong. It wasn't until the smoke cleared, I figured it out." A scoff escaped his control, meant to break the tension, but there was no detachment that could make it better. "Turned out I'd trusted the wrong person. A K-9 agent with the DEA. He'd given us everything we needed to raid. Layout of the compound, how many cartel soldiers would be there, how to find the drugs, but I found out later he'd been taking cartel money for years. We'd been fed bad intel from the start."

Her throat convulsed on a strong swallow. "You knew him?"

"Yeah. I knew him. Bear, too. They were partners since she was a pup, but there was an explosion during the raid. The cartel had known we were coming and constructed IEDs to slow us down. Bear put herself in the line of fire to save her handler, but he didn't make it. She was discharged due to too much head trauma after that." A heaviness he hadn't allowed to take over distracted him from the task at hand.

"That's how you and Bear were partnered?" she asked.

"Seemed fitting. She was already comfortable with me, and I wasn't going to let her be put down." There was more to it than that, but they'd wasted enough time. "Is that the phone?"

Elena dropped her attention to the rag in her hand. "Yeah. I charged it the last time I was here a couple weeks ago. It should have enough power left to get what you…" Unwrapping the package, she revealed a slim, shiny, silver flip phone predating anything that could connect to the internet. Brand new from the look of it. Her panicked gaze shot to his. "I don't understand."

"What's the problem?" he asked.

"This isn't my phone." She shot to her feet. "Someone else has been here."

Chapter Five

Nobody should've known where she'd hidden that phone.

She hadn't told anyone. Not her parents. Not even Deputy McCrae. Without that information, what chances did they have of getting Daniel back?

Acid collected at the back of her throat. Cash had instantly contacted Jocelyn and gone on alert to search the mission, but there'd been nothing to find. Thousands of people visited the pueblos every year. Tourists, Mexican and Native American elders, architecture enthusiasts. This place had felt safe. Just enough out of reach to keep her eight-year-old brother from going through her things but close enough to get to the phone if she needed to run again.

Cash's words lanced through her. *The longer we're here, the higher chances someone reports your movements.* Could someone have followed her out here? Had her ex placed spies throughout town to keep tabs on her every move? Who she talked to, where she went and what she ate for dinner?

She turned the phone meant to look like hers over in her hand. Cash had already gone through it. The contacts list was empty. No sent or received messages. No call log. It was as though someone had tried to replicate her device, bought one, then come back here to make the switch. The only thing they had going for them was the SIM card. Maybe someone in Socorro could trace it back to a credit card purchase. Security companies could do that, right?

But more important, what did this mean for her brother? She hadn't followed through. Socorro and its operatives weren't going to get the intel she promised in return for bringing Daniel home.

The gusts coming through the SUV's windows whipped her hair around her face. A whimper pierced through the endless loop of thoughts tearing her apart bit by bit just before Bear's wet nose prodded the side of her neck from the cargo area. "What happens now?"

Neither Cash nor Jocelyn had said a word since they'd rushed her back to the vehicle, and she wasn't sure they would now. Bone threatened to break through the back of Cash's hand from his grip on the steering wheel. "Now we regroup. Try to come at this another way."

He didn't have to finish that thought. It'd already wedged between her ribs. Every second they wasted trying to pin down *Sangre por Sangre* lowered the chances of them recovering Daniel. This was her fault. She'd been responsible for the information she'd gathered living with her ex for those three months. She should've been more careful. She should've gone out there sooner.

"I remember one of the addresses I saved in the phone." It wasn't much, but it was a start. If they found a connection between the cartel and one location, they might be able to build from there. "Twenty acres of undeveloped property. I remember it because it was one of the addresses I was able to get photos of online. There was nothing out there, from what I could tell, but it seemed odd the cartel would just let it sit."

"Cartels like *Sangre por Sangre* own thousands of acres of undeveloped land." Jocelyn angled her chin over her shoulder, though not enough to get a direct look at Elena. "It makes moving their product—drugs, women and alcohol—easier across the state. Sometimes they're just used for logistics' sake."

It made sense, and of all the operatives Socorro employed, she supposed Jocelyn would be the one whose literal job it was to confirm that theory. But Elena's gut said something different. That the mortgage statements and environmental surveys she'd found for that specific piece of land represented more than a simple route the cartel used to avoid law enforcement. She didn't know why, but it felt important. She ran through the address over and over until it'd be impossible to forget.

All too soon, the SUV dipped into the compound's underground parking garage. Her vision struggled to adjust to the lack of input for a few moments, casting her into a world of darkness. She hadn't actually been conscious for this part when Cash had brought her here, and a thread of anxiety clawed up her throat.

Bear whined from the back seat, her cold nose grazing along Elena's neck, as though seeking comfort. Cash reached overhead, and the interior of the SUV lit up. That simple action not only seemed to calm the dog but took a weight off Elena's chest.

They pulled over in front of a shiny elevator. Jocelyn was the first to exit, before rounding to the back of the vehicle to get Maverick as Elena and Cash hit the asphalt. "I'll check in with Ivy, let her know what we found. Or didn't, rather. I'll keep you up-to-date."

"Thanks, Joce." Cash clicked his tongue, and Bear jumped down from the cargo area. It was sweet. Their relationship. Earlier he hadn't said as much, but she'd guessed Cash and Bear's handler had been close. It must've been hard. Not only to lose that friend but also to realize he'd been responsible for the operation's failure. To uncover that betrayal.

Jocelyn unlocked a door off to the right of the elevator using her keycard and disappeared inside, leaving Cash and Elena alone in the cavernous garage.

Elena didn't really know what would happen next. The intel she'd promised Socorro was missing, her brother was still out there, she wasn't sure if her parents had survived the night and a cartel lieutenant had raided her hometown to find her. Her phone was supposed to fix everything. Now she had nothing. She stared at the replacement. Who'd known about what she'd done? Her ex? One of the men he employed?

"You look like you're about to drop dead." Cash pushed the button for the elevator. The doors parted almost immediately, and he stepped inside. "Let's get you something to eat."

"Yeah." She followed him inside. Because she really didn't have any other choice, did she? She had nothing to go back to. Her ex—and the cartel—had made sure of that. The only thing left to do was find Daniel. The doors slid closed behind her, and she made note of the floor Cash selected. Three.

The phone's plastic protested from the tightness of her grip, catching Bear's attention, and she pocketed it into her borrowed jacket. "Is your dog scared of the dark?"

"Weird, right? I always thought dogs had better vision than we did, but there's something about the dark she doesn't handle well. I have to keep a nightlight on, or she'll whine all night." He scratched behind one of Bear's ears. The dog's jaw loosened as she closed her eyes. Cash slipped the SUV's keys in the right pocket of his cargo pants. "I've asked the vet we keep in-house for the K-9 unit. She has a theory that Bear might've gone temporarily blind from her last concussion. Anytime she can't see, it freaks her out."

Elena knew the feeling. The elevator pinged, letting them out on the same floor she recognized from before. Though this time the tall, dark and scary man beside her wasn't so scary. Cash directed her through the maze of sleek black walls, floors and ceilings until they reached his room. Left. Two rights. Fourth room from the end.

Motioning her inside, Cash stood sentry at the door as she crossed the threshold.

Her movements were subtle and quick. Just as she'd learned living with her ex. She closed the distance between them, nothing more than mere inches keeping her from touching him as she raised her gaze to his. "Thank you, Cash. For everything. If it wasn't for you, Daniel wouldn't have a chance. How am I supposed to repay something like that?"

He studied her from head to toe.

"You've still got a bit of ash and dirt on you. Bathroom's there. Fully stocked. Feel free to shower." His voice was husky, and she couldn't help but feel it rumble through her. "I'll have Jocelyn send over another change of clothes while I grab us something to eat other than a couple old Oreos disguising Bear's allergy medicine."

The aftertaste made a hard comeback at the reminder, and Elena grabbed her stomach to keep it from revolting all over again. She took a step back to find the nearest garbage can. "A toothbrush would also be good."

"You got it, Elle." The hitch at the corner of his mouth that'd twisted her insides earlier exploded into a full-blown smile she hadn't been prepared for. It stole the air from her chest and left her doubting every thought she'd had during the drive back to Socorro. Cash closed the door behind him.

Elle. No one had called her that before. Her family had always called her Lena. The warmth he'd given off evaporated. *Come with me, Lena.* Ice infused her veins despite the sun beaming through the windows. Elena pulled the phone from her pocket and flipped the cover open. The screen lit up. Ten percent battery life. She'd already determined the device had never been used before being shoved inside the mission wall. No reason for anyone to be looking for it then, right?

Pulling up the messaging screen, she entered the only phone number she'd bothered memorizing since she'd returned to Alpine Valley. Hesitation cut through her. If someone had been watching her movements on her ex's orders, reaching out could put her parents in more danger. But not knowing if they were safe was eating at her from the inside. She typed a quick message. Need to meet. You know the place. Tonight.

She sent the message. Cash would be back soon. She had to go now. Elena palmed the SUV's remote key she'd taken from his cargo pants and lunged for the door. Left at the end of the hall. Another left. Then a right. In less than a minute, she faced off with the elevator and hit the call button. Nervous energy had her scanning the floor for signs of Cash, Bear or any of his team. The elevator pinged, and she slipped inside.

She was in the clear. The fist around her heart released. There was no way the cartel was using twenty acres of land for nothing more than a drug route. The chances of finding Daniel there were slim, but she had to try. Her pulse thudded hard at the base of her throat as she locked on to the reflection in the silver doors. The bruises had darkened since last she'd noticed them. One bleeding up her cheek, the other across her opposite temple, but the swelling had at least gone down. She didn't look like she'd gotten into a fight with the end of a rifle.

The overhead lights flickered. Her heart rate skyrocketed out of control at the thought of getting stuck in the dark. The LED light above the door framed out a *G* for garage, and Elena stepped forward in anticipation of getting out of the car as fast as possible.

The doors parted.

The same wall of muscle that'd held her up at the sight of her childhood home burned to the ground blocked her path. Cash. "You know, I'm starting to think you don't like me."

COLOR HAD DRAINED from her face. Like she'd seen a ghost.

Cash only allowed himself a split second of concern before he stretched his hand out. "You're good, but you're not that good."

"You knew." Elena seemed to pull herself back from whatever terror had taken over. Even faced with an obstacle, she wasn't going to let herself crack. Admiration kept a tight hold on his consciousness, but sooner or later, the wall she'd built to keep herself under control was going to fall. He just hoped it didn't get her killed in the process. "Why let me get this far?"

"I wasn't sure of your motivation. Whether you wanted to run or if there was something you were running toward." Her body language didn't come across as nervous. More determined. That challenging gaze flickered behind him, to the fleet of vehicles parked within reach. Elena was gauging her chances of success against him. Wondering if she could outrun him. She couldn't. But, no. She wasn't trying to escape her problems. It wasn't in her genetic makeup. "You're going to that parcel of land your ex tried to hide from you."

A shuddering breath told him everything he needed. "I need to know what's out there. I need to know if that's where my brother is, and I'm not going to stop. You can lock me in your room or order Bear to guard me, but I won't stop trying to leave. I'm not going to sit here while you waste time coming up with an entire mission. Daniel doesn't have days. He needs me now."

Cash had made his decision the moment she'd stepped free from the elevator. Hell, he'd made it long before. Before her promise of inside intel on *Sangre por Sangre* fell through. Back when he'd taken down the bastard who'd intended to abduct her last night. There was nothing he wouldn't do for this woman. Because there was nothing she wouldn't do for those who needed her help, and that deserved respect. He headed for his SUV. "You navigate. I'll drive."

"What?" she asked.

"You got the coordinates, right? You know where we're going." He didn't bother turning around and wrenched the driver's-side door open. "You think there's more to that land than logistics. Let's see what the cartel is hiding."

Because there was no way in hell he was going to let her take on an entire cartel alone.

Elena didn't move to the passenger side of the vehicle, her hand still gripped around the SUV's remote. "What about Bear? I thought you two were inseparable."

"She's already in the back." Cash hauled himself behind the steering wheel and secured himself inside. Waiting. He centered his Rottweiler's face in the rearview mirror. "Up for another assignment?"

Bear licked the tip of her nose and along one side of her mouth in response. No complaints.

He started the engine with a push of a button as Elena climbed into the passenger seat.

"Shouldn't we wait for backup or something?" She slid her palms down the length of her thighs. She'd been prepared to fight him and lose. Not partner with him on a potential dead end. "Does your team know you're doing this?"

"No." Cash shoved the SUV into Drive and launched them from the underground parking garage. Sun cut through the windshield, making the landscape monochromatic and bright. "Best-case scenario, you're right. We find the cartel. If we're spotted and have to engage, I can ping the team for backup. The chopper cuts that down to ten."

"And the worst case?" The weight of each word told him she already knew the answer. "What then?"

"Worst case, you're wrong." He checked the side mirror to focus on something other than the effect her voice had on him. Soothing and compelling. Emotional. Strong. The combination pulled him into a false sense of security and refused to let go. "There's nothing out there. You get whatever this is out of your system, and we come up with a new plan to find your brother."

"Do you trust them? The people you work with?" Elena clutched the SUV's remote tighter, as though it were a lifeline through the violence and deception she'd already survived.

The question was simple enough, but the meaning... That was something else entirely. "You want to know whether or not Socorro will keep their word without you delivering on yours."

"I've been through it a thousand times in my head. No one knew I had that information about my husband's business dealings. And the fact whoever took it knew where I'd hidden it and replaced it with the same model of phone makes me think you were right. That the cartel has been watching me," she said. "I wouldn't blame your boss for believing I'd lied about it to begin with."

She wasn't talking about Ivy. She was talking about him. Cash checked the mirrors to ensure they hadn't been followed. A habit he couldn't afford to quit in his line of work. "You said husband that time. Not ex."

She didn't answer right away, seemingly trying to gauge how much to tell him.

Soldiers who climbed the ranks inside organizations like *Sangre por Sangre* were few and far between. Most had been brought in from right off the street as youths, most likely victims of their own recruitment tactics. They were encouraged to prove themselves at all costs and trained to compete with one another. For food, sleeping arrangements, the clothes on their backs, assignments. To make it as high as a lieutenant, a recruit would have to survive years of mental, physical and emotional abuse, not to mention learn to deliver it out to his subordinates when called for. Including those closest to him.

"You're still married." She'd told him as much, hadn't she? When she'd initially explained she'd run with nothing but a phone the lieutenant didn't know about and the clothes on her back. But the idea she was legally bound to another man set him on edge. Even if she was the one who'd wanted out of the relationship.

Though someone had known about what she'd done. The question was how.

"Hard to get a divorce when one party refuses to sign the papers." Elena directed her attention out the window, hugging herself around the middle as though to keep it together a little bit longer. "Not to mention beats the man who served him the papers to a pulp."

"Your friend the deputy?" he asked.

He barely caught her nod as they carved through a dirt road cutting across the county. There was nothing out here but weeds, dirt and death, yet Cash found himself not wanting to be anywhere else right then.

"He's with the Alpine Valley police department," she said. "Deputy McCrae. He was the one who got me out. He drove all the way to Albuquerque to help me escape, but he barely survived going back. Spent three weeks in an intensive care unit after surgery to relieve a blood clot in his brain. Came out with a shaved head, a four-inch scar and six broken ribs for his trouble. I would do anything to go back and not ask him to deliver those papers, but at the time, it'd felt like the only thing that would finally put an end to this."

But the world didn't work like that. Not with abusers.

"Brock McCrae." His study of Alpine Valley and their limited resources set the name at the front of his mind. The deputy had only been with the department two years. Good record. No reports of abuse of authority or excessive force as far as Cash could remember. Then again, a little town like that didn't usually see anything more serious than misdemeanors, and most of them came from bored teenagers planning to get out as soon as they graduated high school.

Elena turned that guarded gaze to him. "How did you know that?"

"It's my job to know all the players on the board." Big or small. But it hadn't been enough to stop the cartel from raiding and slaughtering a small town in search of their intended target. Elena. The sun arced into the western half of the sky, cutting through the windshield and diminishing his view. "What's so special about this land? Of all the documents you found with all the addresses, why this one?"

She pinched her hands between her knees. "I'm

not sure. I just know what my gut is telling me. It was important. When my…husband learned I'd checked the mail that day—it was the one and only time I saw a mortgage statement pertaining to that location—he was angry. Angrier than I'd ever seen him before."

It was easy enough to fill in the rest of the blanks, and the eighteen-year-old who'd enlisted straight into the Marine Corps after the largest terrorist attack had hit the country went on the defense. "He punished you for it."

"He locked me in our wine cellar for three days." Her voice detached slightly. Not in any big way, but in the smallest change in pitch. A memory she was better off believing had happened to someone else. "No food. No water or way to go to the bathroom. There was no electricity. No light. I clawed at that door, begging him to let me out, but he never came."

Elena brushed her thumb over her middle fingernail, and Cash only then realized it was missing. The base had started growing back some but stood out more than the others. "I can see why Bear might be scared of the dark. I am, too. I have to sleep with a night-light. Ridiculous, right? A grown woman paralyzed by a childish fear like that."

Cash had held himself in check since the moment she'd woken on that examination table in the doc's office. But he couldn't anymore. He reached over the center console and wrapped her hand with the missing fingernail in his. "It's not ridiculous, Elena, and you sure as hell don't let anyone tell you it is. They don't know. Nobody knows what you went through or what you've survived, including me. What I do know? You deserve good things in your life, and I'm going to damn sure be one of them as long as we're partnered together. Whether that means bringing Daniel home or taking down the son of a bitch who hurt you, I will not let you down. Ever. You understand?"

"I understand." A glimmer of tears reflected the afternoon sun as Cash released his hold. She swiped at her face with the back of her hand and sat forward. "Thank you."

Barbed wire fencing took shape through the windshield, cutting across their path, and Cash pulled the SUV off the side of the one-way dirt road. Bear *ruff*ed from the cargo area. Apparently not too pleased with his driving. As usual.

"This is it." Elena leaned forward in her seat. "We're here."

Chapter Six

They didn't have a plan.

She scouted the length of the barbed wire fence through the windshield. There was no gate from what she could tell. At least not for a few acres in each direction. The only reason to use a fence was to keep intruders out. Or someone in.

Elena shoved free of the SUV. Midday sun warmed her skin and instantly beaded sweat at the back of her neck. Shading her eyes, she tried to gauge the distance between them and the opposite border of land. She'd been wrong before. "This is more than twenty acres."

Cash rounded the hood of the vehicle, taking position beside her. "You sure these are the coordinates?"

"Yes, but that was months ago." She hated to think of what this new information meant. More acreage meant having to take more time to search. Time she wasn't sure Daniel had. "Is it possible the cartel has bought up more land?"

"Only one way to find out." He maneuvered to the

back of the SUV and hauled the cargo area door over-head. Bear jumped free, seemingly scanning their sur-roundings for herself, and a bit of relief eased through Elena. From what Cash had told her, Bear trained for things like this. She could sense danger before they stepped into it. Like their personal radar. Cash extracted a large set of bolt cutters from the cargo area and tossed them on the ground. He released the magazine from his sidearm and checked the bullets inside, then slammed it back into place. In seconds, he'd locked the vehicle and presented her with the bolt cutters. "You know what this means, don't you? We're about to trespass on cartel land. Your ex's land. Once we cross that line, there's no going back. No more running."

He was giving her a choice. Either confront her ex to save her brother or go back and put the past behind her as she'd intended. But it wasn't really a choice at all. Not for her. Elena accepted the bolt cutters, sur-prised at the weight. "I understand."

"Let's do this." He followed her to the fence, his massive body shading her from the sun.

Elena centered the bolt cutters against one link and clamped down. The metal broke as easily as uncooked angel-hair pasta. Daniel's favorite snack whenever she caught him in the pantry. She repeated the process until an uneven section of fence separated from the main frame—too loud in the silence of the desert.

"Ladies first." Cash held the section of fence back as she crawled through with the bolt cutters, then followed far more gracefully than she'd ever managed. "We stick to the fence. Scout the perimeter. If anything happens, we can get out fast. This is surveillance only, Elena. We see something, we call for backup. We do not engage. Agreed?"

Her heart threatened to override logic. "What if we find him?"

"The odds of your brother's survival are better if the entirety of Socorro has our back." He was waiting for her to agree to his terms. Wondering if he could count on her in a sticky situation. Because the last time he'd trusted the wrong person during an assignment, he'd lost someone important to him and gained Bear in the process.

She wasn't a soldier. She didn't have a weapon other than an oversize pair of bolt cutters, not to mention none of his training. He was the expert here, and deep down, she understood his number one priority would be getting her out alive if faced with danger. "Okay."

"Watch where you're stepping. Scorpions and snakes are faster than you think." Cash took the first step, leading them along the fence. He kept pace as easily as if they were on a stroll along a cemented sidewalk instead of navigating loose rock, weeds and potential threats from wildlife. Not to mention armed gunmen who'd given up their morals a long time ago.

Bear jogged alongside her master, snout to the ground, with Elena taking up the rear of their little search party. The fence rattled with a gust of wind and stripped her nerves raw. Her mouth watered at the sudden intensity of the sun overhead. It was searing the skin of her scalp where her hair parted down the middle.

She shouldn't be out here.

Twenty-four hours ago, she'd been living an entirely different life. Recovering from her marriage at home, with her family, secure in knowing she could unravel her ex at a moment's notice if provoked.

Now her parents were missing, her brother had been taken and the information she'd risked her life for had been stolen. There was nothing left. Nothing but a Rottweiler and her grumpy, sarcastic handler in the middle of a desert determined to swallow her whole. And, somehow, they'd become her only comfort. "Who was he? Bear's first handler. You said you knew him. Were you friends?"

"His name was Wade." Cash refused take his eye off the path up ahead. It was easy to imagine him dressed in his combat uniform. Solely focused on the task at hand. That kind of intensity had transferred into his new life. One ripped apart by betrayal and loss. Just like hers. "He was my brother."

Her step hitched, but Cash didn't seem to notice. "Your brother. As in—"

"Same parents." His voice shifted down. Most likely unnoticeable to anyone else, but in the time since he'd saved her life, she'd become acutely aware of each and every change in his demeanor. "I'm older by eleven months. We enlisted around the same time. Right after September 11. I remember that day so clearly. He'd just graduated high school. I was still trying to figure out my life—what I wanted to do. We were sitting in front of the television, watching the whole thing play out, and we just looked at each other. We knew right then and there what we were meant to do. Next day, I went down to the Marine Corps recruitment office. Within five years, I ended up one of the top weapons experts and strategists. Wade went into the army for intelligence."

"That's how he ended up with the DEA?" Elena hadn't missed the part where the Meyers brothers had instantly responded to an explosive need for help when the country needed them most. It was what Cash had done last night. Charging into an unknown situation for the sake of a stranger. It was admirable, ethical and, in her opinion, one of the greatest sacrifices someone could make for another. And he'd made it for her. "Gathering information against the cartels?"

"Was damn good at it, too. He wasn't like other

analysts. Didn't like sitting behind a desk, punching in data for eight hours a day. He wanted to be in the field, investigating the tips he got himself before sending them up the ladder. Made a hell of a case vetting all the intel himself. Managed to convince the higher-ups to keep him and Bear in the field. Within a few weeks, the DEA had actionable intelligence to tear apart the Colombian cartel. Watch your step." Cash pointed out a scorpion the size of her fist, hidden by its near translucency against the desert floor. "At least on paper."

"But he started taking money from the very people he was supposed to be fighting." She craned her head back over her shoulder, searching the flat, dead landscape for something—anything—to confirm they were in the right place. That she hadn't made another mistake.

"I don't know where it went wrong." A heaviness she'd come to hate tainted his words. "Wade wasn't a gambler. Didn't have financial issues as far as I could tell. Wasn't in over his head on his house or in debt. He didn't need their money. Best I can guess, they threatened someone close to him."

"You." It made sense. While *Sangre por Sangre* didn't hail from Colombia, their tactics overlapped in more than a few areas. Personal relationships would always be an easy target, and from what she'd learned of Cash, she bet Wade Meyers would do whatever it took to protect the people he cared about. Her heart hurt at the idea. Because in much the same way, they were in similar positions. Him with his brother. Her with Daniel.

"Yeah." Cash left it at that.

They walked several hundred more feet along the perimeter in silence. She wasn't sure how much distance they'd covered, but the backs of her thighs had started protesting the uneven terrain.

"Platz," he said.

It took her brain too long to process Cash's sudden command. Faster than she thought possible, his body encapsulated hers. He tugged her to sit against him, her back to his front, behind a large brittlebush. Bear dove for another section in the bush, then sat absolutely still. Cash practically melted into the leaves, enough for them to prod at her overheated skin as yellow flowers closed in around her vision. Her breath puffed too hard out of her chest as she listened. "What is it?"

"Shh." He unholstered his weapon. His arm was still gripped around her waist. Solid and warm.

The sound of footsteps crunched from a few feet away. Goose bumps rippled down her exposed arms as a shadow crawled in front of them from the opposite side of the bush. Elena reached for the bolt cutters she'd dropped, but Cash laid his hand over hers.

Static breached through the protective layer of

brush, and the shadow's arm shifted upward toward the head. *"No hay nada aquí."* There's nothing out here. *"Me dirijo de vuelta."* I'm headed back.

Her chest threatened to explode from holding her breath, but Cash's hold remained on her. Grounded, strong. It shouldn't have meant anything in that moment—especially given the danger they were in—but his touch was the only thing keeping her from spiraling.

The shadow eased away from them, but even then, Cash waited a few seconds before releasing her. "Slowly."

She tipped her balance forward and crawled on all fours into the open. No sign of the man, but a scuff of boot prints encircled the opposite side of the bush. They were in the clear. For now. "Just so you're aware, I don't take German commands."

"If I hadn't told Bear to get down, she'd have given us away." The dog crawled free of her hiding spot as though she understood Cash's every word. He holstered his weapon. "I wasn't worried about you."

"Oh." His words shouldn't have wounded her at all, but she couldn't help but twist his meaning into something along the lines of not caring for her at all. It was silly, really. After what he'd done for her, she knew better. But the effects of her marriage had yet to wear off. "Why do you think he was out here? We haven't seen anything since we left the car."

Cash nodded northeast, directing her attention to

the half-built structure at the bottom of a man-made valley she hadn't seen until right then. "I think he's guarding that."

ELENA HAD BEEN RIGHT.

Which meant his and Socorro's attempts to track and gauge *Sangre por Sangre*'s movements and assets had failed.

The compound was bigger than anything he'd seen. Constructed from massive resources no amount of inside intel had tipped them off to. Dug deep into the earth, half of the structure peeked out between mountains of dirt shoved to the side. Haulers and excavators worked in slow motion as Cash added up the number of armed men patrolling the perimeter of the site.

Cash had jogged back to the SUV for his gear. Lowering the binoculars, he handed them off to Elena, who was flat on her stomach beside him. He'd always worked alone during his missions. Analyze the threat. Report to Ivy. It was kind of nice to have someone who didn't bark back. Though that feeling didn't stay long. "I count thirty-five armed, six excavator drivers and at least thirteen others."

"You think they all work for the cartel?" She pressed the binoculars against her eyes.

"Organizations like *Sangre por Sangre* don't let outsiders in. Either they're in the ranks, or fated to die once they finish the job," he said.

"I can't believe nobody knew this was out here. The building has to be at least double the size of Socorro headquarters. This kind of project has to come with environmental reports and permits." She lowered the binoculars as though trying to take it all in with her own eyes. "You and your team really had no idea what they've been building?"

"No." A mistake he seemed destined to repeat at every juncture. Cartels operated out in the open. They took credit for attacks and assassinations. A project like this didn't fall into normal operating procedure. What the hell was going on here? "My guess—this place doesn't exist on paper. Wouldn't be surprised if the cartel paid off the right people or threatened or murdered whoever they needed to to keep it under the radar."

"What is it for?" she asked. "Why go through all the trouble?"

"A headquarters. See those piles of dirt?" Cash moved along the barely-there ridge providing cover for their positions. Bear had been on enough of these scouting missions to keep her head low and stay put. But Elena… She wasn't trained for this. She didn't understand the rules of warfare. She was just a victim caught in the cross fire. "They're going to bury the building once construction is complete. Satellite imagery over this area would just register the dirt. The building will give off heat, but combined with the desert, there won't be anything to differentiate the different sources. Within a year, the weeds will be back, and this place will be completely hidden in plain sight. *Sangre por Sangre* has always been left to operate under the banner of their lieutenants across the state. This will give them a place to create a stronghold."

"Unless we stop them." Elena handed back the binoculars. "Look. The backside of the building is already finished. There aren't any guards patrolling over there. We could probably circle around and drop down."

"Assuming there's a way to get inside from there." He'd known this was coming. The moment they'd crossed the site, she would've already come up with a way to get inside. "Elena, we had an agreement. Surveillance only."

"My brother could be in there." Desperation and a hint of anger solidified her expression. "Doesn't your entire organization exist for the sole purpose of dismantling the cartel? What better way than to catch them off guard? To hit them on their own turf?"

There was no reasoning with her. She'd already made up her mind.

"I'm not saying we leave and forget this place exists." The numbers weren't adding up. They were outmanned, outgunned and working blind. "We need a layout of the building, confirmation your brother is here and support—preferably more than thirteen bullets and a dog scared of the dark. We have no idea what we're walking into down there."

Bear craned her head toward them.

"Don't pretend you aren't." He hadn't meant to be so harsh, but this situation was coming dangerously close to the DEA operation that'd gone to hell and taken his brother. The intel they'd been relying on had turned out to be nothing but wishful thinking. He couldn't go through that again.

"He's here. I know he is, and I've waited long enough." She backed away from the ridge overlooking the construction site and shoved to stand. "You can wait for your team, but I'm not letting Daniel suffer one more second wondering if someone is coming for him."

Dirt kicked up at her heels as she raced along the barbed fence.

Bear's whine reflected the war tearing through Cash. He couldn't let Elena go in there without backup. Let alone unarmed.

"Does she think bolt cutters are a weapon?" Bear didn't have an answer for him. Cash dragged himself away from the ridge, keeping low as he followed in Elena's footsteps. Her frame shrank the faster she ran. He whistled low to call for Bear and slowed long enough to trigger the emergency signal on her collar. No matter where they were, the team would respond to the call. "Damn it."

He just hoped it was in time.

Battle-ready tension infiltrated the muscles along his neck and shoulders as Elena slid down the incline behind the compound. Dust funneled overhead, practically signaling anyone within a mile radius of her presence, but the soldiers and workers in the basin somehow hadn't noticed. Cash picked up the pace. Rock and dirt penetrated through his gear down the slope. The earth wall threatened to swallow him and Bear whole as his view of the site cut off. Solid ground caught them at the bottom and dragged Elena's attention from a set of double doors at the back of the structure.

He crossed the dry, cracked distance between them. Every cell in his body wanted the reassurance of her touch again—to make sure she was okay—but they were living on borrowed time as it was.

"What are you doing? Go back. Wait for your team." Surprise softened the curve of her mouth and dropped her hands away from a keycard panel installed beside the entrance.

"Couldn't let you have all the fun, now, could I?" He nodded to the panel. Top-of-the-line security. No access in or out without a corresponding keycard. But, being employed by one of the brand's installers, he'd come across this model before. And the bypass built into the system. "Watch out."

Cash entered a six-digit code. The panel LEDs lit up green and released the dead bolts securing both doors.

"How did you do that?" she asked.

"Socorro is one of two companies certified to install this brand of security system, but it turns out the override code is the same." He unholstered his weapon, setting Bear at full alert. "We have no idea what's waiting on the other side of these doors. Stay behind me. Use me as a shield if you have to. Bear will protect you if someone gets close enough, but there's no way for her to stop a bullet."

He crouched beside Bear and removed her emergency collar. "Anything happens to me, get out and put as much distance between you and this place as you can. The team can find you with this."

Elena pocketed Bear's collar and gripped both handles of the bolt cutters in front of her, nodding. "I'm ready."

She wasn't. Very few people who hadn't seen war could be ready for a situation like this, and letting her walk right into the enemy's hands was out of the question.

Cash wrenched open the nearest door and took aim. One foot in front of the other, he scanned the long hallway from left to right. No movement. No ambush waiting for them to cross the threshold. Cement walls tunneled ahead of them. The compound itself was still under construction, but overhead fluorescent lights had been installed in equal distance, lighting their way. "They're already up and running."

"How is that possible? Half of the building is a gaping hole." Elena's arm brushed against his shoulder.

He didn't know, but if the compound already had power, it stood to reason that *Sangre por Sangre* was further ahead on the project than he'd initially estimated. Like the Death Star. Cash moved along the wall, Bear taking up the rear, Elena sandwiched between them. *"Pass auf."*

His canine partner huffed confirmation, her nails clicking against the cement tomb they'd infiltrated. She'd guard Elena with her life if necessary.

But the place was a ghost town. No cameras in sight. No guards or offices in this section of hallway. None of this made sense. Why install lights and a security system if there was nothing here to protect?

His instincts provided the answer, and Cash pulled up short. "We need to get out of here."

"What? No." Elena refused to budge. "We have to find—"

Bear growled low in her chest, the sound echoing off the walls closing in around them.

He took aim at empty space along the corridor, but something was down there. Something that rivaled his human senses.

The power cut out. Bear whimpered from the tail end of their search party. Her fear of the dark would override any command he gave, and without her to protect Elena, he was operating blind. They had to get out of here. This whole plan had been a setup from the beginning. Just like before.

"Damn." Cash grabbed for his flashlight. He hit the power button. "Back up. Head for the door."

Elena's hand fisted around the shoulder of his Kevlar vest. Her gasp reached his ears as a single face emerged in the beam.

"Please. Don't rush out on my account," the man said. "I've been waiting a long time for my wife to come home."

The lights flickered to life, revealing the circle of armed men surrounding them from every angle. Including their exit. How was that possible? How could he have been so blind? He'd walked them right into an ambush.

"I'm not your wife." Elena's confidence embedded deep in his chest. Almost enough to convince him they might have a chance here. "You can't be married to someone who only exists on paper."

Physical tension pinched the man's mouth into a thin line. Like the guy had just eaten a bunch of sour grapes. Elena had hit her mark. "Take them."

The circle surrounding them tightened.

"Touch her, and you'll lose your hand." Cash gripped his weapon tighter as though the simple action would ensure their escape, but the truth was they were nothing against a small army. They weren't getting out of this without a few scars.

Bear's yip had him turning to amputate whoever'd put a hand on her.

Pain exploded at the back of his head. Lightning blinded him for a fraction of a second. Then darkness.

Elena's scream followed him into unconsciousness. "Cash!"

Chapter Seven

The rope was too tight.

Elena dragged her chin away from her chest. The fibers around her wrists scratched at oversensitive skin. A dull thud pounded at the back of her head, but all she could think about was the binding contorting her arms behind her back. Which didn't make sense. She should be far more concerned with a head injury than any damage done to her wrists. Was that a sign of a head injury? She didn't know.

She forced her eyes open, fighting the drug of unconsciousness. Her heart pumped blood too fast as she took in the darkness. There were no shapes to make out. No noise to distinguish through the pulse behind her ears. Her throat convulsed to fill the silence, but she was paralyzed against the inky blackness closing in. A weak sound escaped instead. Grating. Pathetic.

He was punishing her again.

How long this time? Four days? More? She didn't

know this room. It wasn't part of her own home this time. She couldn't see the door or make out a way to escape. But, knowing her husband, there would be no way to escape. There hadn't been the last time.

Pulling at the rope, she struggled to contain the tears burning in her eyes. No. No, no, no. This couldn't be happening. Her ankles had been secured. This wasn't punishment. This was domination. She hadn't obeyed, and he was going to make her pay.

It took everything she had to take her next breath, only one name forming in the sobbing inhale. "Cash?"

Movement provoked her senses from a few feet away.

A spark of hope zinged through her, and for the first time since she'd opened her eyes, her shoulders relaxed away from her ears. He was here. He'd get them out of this. She had to believe that. Because he was her only option.

"Did you really think you could just walk away from me, Elena?" he asked. "That I wouldn't find you?"

Dread pooled in the pit of her stomach. Not Cash. That voice had woken her in the middle of the night for months, even after she'd left it behind. Elena pressed her back into the chair he'd secured her to. She still couldn't see him, and her hands immediately worked to free herself and put as much distance between them as possible.

Warm light reached for the ceiling and spread

throughout the room at the pull of a string. It was a desk lamp, illuminating every cinder block wall and a single entrance. And beside it, her husband. He was looking tired. Too thin. Stressed? Though still handsome. His dark hair, peppered with silver at his temples, didn't come close to showing his age as much as the exhaustion around his eyes. His once terra-cotta skin tone had paled slightly. Not enough sun. A troll guarding his mountain of treasure. The white suit paired with a black button-down shirt had starred in many of her nightmares since escaping. He was everything she remembered and everything she wanted to forget.

"Where is my brother?" Fear threatened to bleed into her voice, but she wouldn't give him the satisfaction. She wasn't that woman anymore. The one he'd targeted, seduced, lied to and betrayed. She wasn't his plaything that he got to bring out whenever he got bored. "Where's Cash?"

Her husband slid off the edge of the desk, smoothing invisible wrinkles from his suit. In truth, she'd never seen the slightest flaw in his appearance, even in sleep. It would only take away from his presumed power. "Come now. We don't need to talk about that. You must've missed me. I certainly missed you."

Spreading his arms in front of him, the man she'd known as Metias Leyva—the one who'd asked her to take his last name—waited there as though she would stand up and walk right to him. As though he hadn't had his men knock her unconscious and tie her to a chair in the dark.

She wasn't sure how long she'd been out. How much time she'd wasted. How much time Daniel had left. "You can't miss someone you didn't know."

"That again? We've talked about this, *mi amor*." His laugh broke over the room. Like she'd recounted a joke she'd heard rather than the dysfunction of the life they'd tried to build together. He dragged a chair matching hers from beneath the desk with the lamp, and it was then she realized this room didn't have any windows. He'd trapped her in what seemed to be an office. Underground. Metias took his seat across from her, his knees brushing against hers. He'd done it on purpose. To remind her he was the one who had control. That she was at his mercy. As she always would be. "Do you remember what I told you the last time you were in a room like this?"

The memories were there on the cusp of her mind. At the ready to unravel her from the inside, but Elena wasn't going to break. Not here. And not for him. "Hard to forget the first time your husband locks you in a dark room for three days without food or water."

Eyes the color of dark chocolate—compelling and deep and fluid—centered on her and triggered her defenses. He set his palms on the top of her thighs and leaned in. A hint of his aftershave, the one she used to love, worked into her system. His hands were warm. Deceiving in so many ways. "I told you my work requires an extra layer of security. My associates wouldn't hesitate to take you from me if I made a mistake. Neither would the government of this country. Lying to you—it was the only way I knew how to protect you."

She'd heard this speech before. In that cellar after she'd lost her voice from screaming and her insides were trying to eat themselves. At the time, she would've agreed to anything he said to get the relief she'd desperately craved. She would've done anything. But time and distance and freedom had changed her. "Your work. You mean abducting children and turning them into soldiers, killing innocent people, destroying their homes and pushing them out of their towns. Running drugs and women and guns? That work? The work you chose over our marriage time and again. You didn't lie to me to protect me, Metias. You lied because you were scared I would see you for who you really are. A monster."

He moved so fast, she didn't have time to brace herself first.

The strike twisted her head over her left shoulder and stung across her face. Her eyes watered from the impact, but there wasn't a single bone in her body that regretted what she'd said. He stood and pulled the chair back where he'd taken it from. Turning back, Metias tugged a handkerchief from his pocket and wiped his hand clean. Couldn't leave any evidence connecting him to his atrocities. That wouldn't bode well for his work or the people he worked for, now, would it? "What happened to Alpine Valley was your fault, *mi amor*. I gave you everything. A home, clothing, food on our table. I pulled you from poverty in that nothing town and introduced you to a better life. This is how you repay me? By stealing information about my business and running away?"

He knew what she'd taken. How? For how long? She'd been so careful. Blood beaded at the corner of her mouth. She moved to swipe it away, but the rope had somehow grown tighter around her wrists. His wedding ring, the same ring she'd slipped onto his hand that day in the church surrounded by her family and friends, had busted her lip. The people he'd isolated her away from, that'd given up on trying to keep in touch. She wouldn't lick it away. She'd make him see it. See the kind of man he'd become. "That's the problem, Metias. A marriage isn't a debt to be repaid. It's a partnership—a relationship that requires give and take. But the only relationship you'll ever be able to count on in the future is the one with your hand."

That crooked smirk he intentionally used to make her feel less than human graced her with its presence, and her confidence waned. Scrubbing a hand through the beard scruff showing more salt than pepper these days, Metias shoved his opposite hand into his pants' pocket. His knuckles fought against the fabric there, as though he were wrapping his fingers around something. He rounded behind her, out of sight, and she found herself hating the idea of not being able to see him rather than confronting him head-on as she'd prepared for all these months. "You asked me before where your brother was. Strong *chico*, that one. A fighter. I knew it the moment I met him. Could see it in his eyes. You and he share that trait. You both endure physical punishment well."

What? What did that mean? Elena struggled to catch her breath. "What have you done? Where is Daniel?"

Metias penetrated her peripheral vision, a phone in his hand. A low whoosh registered. A message? "But that means you also share the same weakness. So here's what I'm going to do, Elena."

The door across the room swung inward. A man—familiar even through the dim lighting of the desk lamp—filled the doorway with mountainous muscle and an obvious pride, as though he'd just won killer of the year three years in a row. It was him. The one she'd suspected had been assigned to follow her through Albuquerque any day she dared leave the house alone. She hadn't been able to get proof before. Not with her husband's knack for hiding any real pieces of their life from her. Now she knew.

"I'm only going to give you one more chance."

Metias moved to wipe the blood from her mouth with his thumb, and wasn't that the perfect example of the man she'd once trusted to love her, to care about her? Never one to lower himself for the benefit of others. He locked on to her chin as she jerked away from his touch, pinching her mouth in his grip. "Apologize for what you've done. Forget about the man you dragged into this mess you've made and come home. Be my wife. Not behind me as before, but at my side. Where you belong."

Cash. Her heart threatened to suction inside out. He'd taken a brutal hit to the head with the butt of the soldier's gun, and her face ached in remembrance of where Metias's gunman had done the same to her. She'd watched him drop so hard, she feared he might never wake up. And Bear… The Rottweiler had tried to protect them by going after Metias. And failed. It was up to Elena to save them now. Because Metias was right in a way. She'd gotten them into this mess. "And if I refuse?"

She already knew the answer. It'd lodged in her chest the moment Daniel had been taken from her.

Her husband leveraged both hands on the chair arms, boxing her within his broad frame. "Then you'll lose Daniel forever. And I'll finish burning Alpine Valley and everyone in it to the ground."

THE TWELFTH HIT must've cracked a rib.

Cash's body swung backward from the momentum. He could barely see out of his left eye from the swelling. The cartel didn't condone trespassing. He'd be lucky if that broken rib didn't puncture his lung before the night was over.

"Who do you work for?" The soldier who'd turned him into a life-size piñata wasn't going to wait for an answer. He hadn't yet. The thirteenth strike cut a jagged ridge over Cash's eyebrow. *"Policia?"*

Stinging pain enveloped his face. He dropped his head back between his strung-up hands in an attempt to numb the pain, but the relief never came. It wouldn't. Not until he had eyes on Elena and Bear. But the chances of getting out of the makeshift cell they'd hoisted him into weren't in his favor. Not without his gear or weapons. The building itself was new, but a hint of human decomposition stained the air of what looked to be a gym pieced together with mismatched machines, barbells and dumbbells. Sweat, and blood and horror. He wasn't the cartel's first visitor to this area, and he certainly wouldn't be the last.

"No, man. He's not police. He came for the boss's woman." The fourteenth hit struck harder than the previous ones. Blood bloomed from a laceration inside his mouth as another soldier took his turn. He backed up, letting Cash swing freely. As though he were the one completely in control. "Big mistake, *vato*. Boss already laid his claim. There ain't nothing you can do now. When he's done with her, she won't even remember your name."

Elena. He'd given his word her ex wouldn't lay another hand on her, and he'd failed. Her and Daniel. This place was a massive maze. Meant to confuse and disorient anyone who wasn't supposed to be here. Law enforcement, military, hostages. It'd take days to search without a guide or a map. Lucky for him, he had his pick. Cash muttered something under his breath.

"What was that?" A soldier who'd gotten a few good punches in stepped forward, but they'd been scattered. No focus. Just intensity. "You begging for your life already? Damn, I lose the bet."

His mouth moved, but Cash didn't let sound leave.

The soldier came closer. Close enough to make contact.

Cash dropped his head back again. Then snapped it forward. His forehead slammed into the soldier's, and the recruit dropped hard with a hand to his nose. Trying to keep the blood in. Wouldn't work.

The laughs died in an instant. Surprise and confusion rippled through the cell.

Anger radiated off the kid. Couldn't be any more than twenty. But Elena's husband had left the soldier with a hostage, which meant the *vato* puckering his shoulders up by his ears had earned the lieutenant's trust over years of service. A child soldier. And while Cash hadn't seen a photo of Daniel, it was all too easy to imagine Elena's brother becoming the one thing she feared most.

Five hostiles. Presumably all armed. Little to no combat experience, but dangerous as a pack all the same. Like wolves. One alpha. The rest were followers but each was capable of defending themselves or taking down their prey alone.

The kid pulled a knife, blood dripping into his mouth and down his shirt. Harsh fluorescent lighting bounced off the blade. "You think you're funny, *cabrón*? Let me wipe that smile off your face, but before I do, I'll take that dog of yours and turn her inside out."

They wouldn't touch Bear.

Mostly because she'd eat any man alive before she let them close.

"Then let's get this over with." The words left his throat as more growl than English.

The recruit stabbed at him.

Cash twisted enough to avoid the soldier's lunge. The blade cut through his T-shirt at his low back, but the kid hadn't calculated his own momentum and met the cement face-first. Cash wrenched his upper body around as another attacker raced forward. He locked his legs around the soldier's neck and squeezed.

Two more moved in, a third staying on the peripheral.

He jerked his legs as hard as possible and choked out the fighter under his grip to take on the next two. Only he wasn't fast enough. One slammed into his gut. Air crushed from his lungs. The impact left him guessing which way was up as his binds broke free of the hook hanging down from the ceiling. His spine wrapped around the soldier he'd knocked out like a damn piece of Play-Doh, but Cash didn't have time to pull himself back together. He wrenched free of the ropes and hauled himself to his feet.

The fourth attacker came from behind. He locked Cash's arms to his side as the one with the knife got his bearings. A swipe of that blade cut through the front of his shirt and scored across his chest. Cash launched his elbow back into the bastard's face behind him. Then he kicked the knee out of the guy in front. A scream filled the small cell and echoed down the corridor.

The soldier at his back—roughly Cash's size—war cried a split second before the son of a bitch practically picked Cash up and hauled him back. They hit the floor together. Before he had a chance to catch his breath, two more attackers were dragging him across the floor by the legs. Cash reached for the closest thing resembling a weapon as he could get: a freestanding dumbbell.

He swung it with everything he had into one man's kneecap. The sickening crunch of shattering bone filled his ears, and he knew then the soldier would never walk right again. Without any use, the cartel would put him down. His attacker dropped to both knees, and Cash ripped the metal across the soldier's face. Another caught him around the middle from out of nowhere. He brought the dumbbell down as hard as he could.

A weight bench slammed into him from behind. He launched forward, saved from eating the floor by the weight in his hand. Cash caught himself against the wall and chucked the dumbbell at the abductor getting ready to throw the bench at his head. The soldier took the weight to the gut and dropped the bench on himself. Cash rotated his shoulder. "I've gotta get in better shape."

A fist rocketed into his face from out of nowhere. He spun into the fifth soldier who'd decided to get in the game and launched his knuckles into the man's jaw. It was a brawl with no end. He knocked one down and another got up, and he was quickly running out of adrenaline.

Strong hands shoved him backward, and he tripped over an unconscious body. His elbow slammed against the cement as he rolled his legs up and over his shoulders to keep him moving. Out of breath, he raised both hands in preparation of what came next. Only one soldier remained. The one who'd locked his arms back while letting the others see if a bunch of candy would break out of him if they hit hard enough.

Cash had misjudged the soldier's size. They weren't equal. If anything, the man had at least fifty pounds of hard muscle on him. No shot caller. Not one to make decisions. His job was meant to keep others in line. "Let me guess. They call you Tiny."

A broken-toothed smile soaked in blood flashed wide. Groans filtered through the hard pound of Cash's pulse behind his ears. Tiny came in for a right hook. Cash ducked and struck the soft tissue of the bastard's organs. Didn't make a damn bit of difference. A thick hand wrapped around Cash's throat and bent him over a stack of barbell weights at his back. Cash dug his grip into the soldier's forearm, then his elbow. Black dots floated across his vision. He had a minute. Maybe seconds.

He hauled his bloodied fist into the soldier's eye, but Tiny recovered too quickly.

His attacker locked his gaze on him. Then thrust his forehead directly into Cash's face.

The world threatened to rip straight out from under him. The black dots took over, his lungs empty. He'd taken on an entire army in hopes of getting Elena and Bear out of here. Instead, they'd be the ones looking down on his body.

Tiny threaded an arm between Cash's legs and hauled him overhead. Gravity took hold, and in a classic wrestling maneuver, the soldier deposited him onto the floor. The collision finished the job the others had started on his ribs.

He had nothing left. Nothing left to fight. Nothing for Elena or her brother.

Pain exploded across his scalp as Tiny fisted a

chunk of his hair. Bone threatened to break under another strike to the face. Once. Twice. His head snapped back into the metal foot of the weight rack, and the world exploded into color. White, yellow and that drugging black he'd followed down the rabbit hole once before. In that pale rainbow, a face materialized. One he felt he'd known his entire life, yet had just encountered less than two days ago. He wanted nothing more than that face to be real. To feel how soft her skin was, to get lost in her warmth, to have those dark brown eyes look at him with something other than fear. To have her believe he was the good guy. That his brother's betrayal didn't run in his veins. Two days. That was all it'd taken for her to remind him of his purpose.

An outline shifted above him, and Cash's hand seemed to move of its own accord in survival mode. He clutched one of the stack weights and brought it forward. A scream nearly punctured his eardrums as Tiny's hand folded as easily as a dish towel against the steel. No. He wasn't giving up. There was something deep down that wouldn't let him—a drive to make this right. He'd given Elena his word that he'd bring her brother home, and that was exactly what he was going to do. Whether he was dead or alive for their reunion.

Cash struggled to his feet. Blood dripped from his mouth, adding to the stains already taking over the cement. The four other soldiers were down for the count, and they wouldn't be getting back up. He grabbed Tiny by the hair and pried the man's head back on his shoulders. "You're going to tell me where you're keeping my dog. Then you and I are going on a field trip."

Chapter Eight

She could feel him staring at her. The man Metias had left behind to watch her.

I have a matter that needs attending to. I'll give you some time to think about my offer. Her husband had kissed her forehead then, as though merely telling her he'd be late for dinner, and closed the door behind him. The unspoken warning in his tone filtered through her head on a loop. He'd given her time, but patience had never been one of his virtues.

She could either run back to him—submissive, apologetic and weak—or lose her brother forever.

And Cash… Where was Cash? Where was Bear? Were they still alive? Part of her had lit up at the possibility that the matter Metias needed to attend to involved the private military contractor and his Rottweiler giving the cartel hell. Cash would fight. In the limited amount of time they'd known each other, she knew that much. An internal mission drove him to overcome any situation—especially any that involved his K-9 companion—but what that meant for Elena, she didn't know. Would their deal still matter to him here? On the surface, she wasn't in physical danger. Metias wouldn't outright kill her for escaping their marriage. But if she refused to return to his side, would that give him reason to add her to the list of dead at his hands?

Her body ached. The ropes around her wrists had cut through skin and were rubbing her raw from the tension. Every move Elena made, every sound, was being catalogued by the brute guarding the door, but she couldn't stay here.

Because she'd already made her decision.

She'd made it the night she'd run from that house. Metias hadn't expected that of her. He'd been counting on her being too weak from starvation and dehydration and fear. That was why he'd agreed to let her have a few minutes of privacy to wash away the blood, sweat and tears from three days in that cellar. He hadn't counted on her climbing through the window, contacting someone for help or avoiding the perimeter patrol of men he'd set to keep the unwanted out.

She wasn't going back.

But that left Daniel at the mercy of a man who didn't have a compassionate bone in his body. A man who would want to keep his leverage as close as possible.

Elena scanned the bunker office for the dozenth

time. Metias had left the lamp on. He'd given her that much, at least. Books, a desk, the chair. None of it would help her out of these ropes. But something like a pen or a letter opener would do. She just had to give herself the opportunity to search. A fresh water bottle, complete with beaded condensation running the length of the plastic, stared back at her from the desk. Her husband would've placed it there on purpose. To break her, to remind her that her life was once again in his hands.

She'd surrendered her power for the chance of a family and a new life outside of Alpine Valley. She'd betrayed herself, but knowing Daniel's life depended on her, knowing Cash and Bear would do whatever it took to see this through, it was time for her to take it all back. To stop hiding. Stop playing the role of victim. To take a stand against the virus infecting the town and people she cared about.

Sizing up the massive boulder-sized man ahead of her, she cleared her throat. There wasn't any scenario in which she'd be able to overcome him physically, but she didn't have to. All she had to do was outsmart him. She'd done it with Metias. She could do it with a guard. Elena nodded toward the bottled water sweating against the desk. "Could I have some water?"

He didn't answer. Didn't even seem to comprehend her question for a series of moments. Maybe considering the repercussions if he gave in to her request, then those of not giving in. Would Metias want him to give her water or not?

She licked her lips, drawing his attention to her mouth. Her voice softened at the slightest provocation. "I'm really thirsty. I won't tell him, if that's what you're worried about. I just… I can't think when my throat is so dry, and he wants an answer soon."

He gruffed and hiked his shoulders a bit higher, which exaggerated the tendons fighting for release along his neck. He wasn't like the others she'd met when Metias threw his parties and forced her to mingle with his friends. Most, if not all of them, came from the same handwoven rug as she did—umber skin, dark hair, even darker eyes. Sweat built along his skin that suggested they shared some kind of ancestry, but the guard's eyes pinched at the edges slightly. More Asian than Mexican. Out of place in *Sangre por Sangre*. Trying to fit in.

He didn't respond. For the stretch of what felt like two full minutes, her plea died between them, but then…he was reaching for the water bottle. Small ticks around his jaw testified of the internal battle waging inside his head. He still wasn't sure he was making the right choice, but Elena couldn't think about what would happen to him after she escaped. Not right then.

Survival. She was good at that.

The guard closed the distance between them and unscrewed the lid. Offering it to her, he set the screw threads against her lower lip and tipped the bottle upward. Liquid drenched the front of her clothing and settled between her thighs.

As she'd intended. She pulled back. "I can't... I can't drink this without my hands. I need the ropes off."

The battle contorted into outright war across his expression. This was the moment that would decide her life. He knew the risks. She saw it in his face. If he let her free, his boss would punish him. If he let her become delirious from dehydration, his boss would punish him. There was no right answer. Every choice ended with a consequence, but he needed to decide which one.

"Please," she said. "You know what he's going to do to me. To my brother."

She wasn't asking him for water. He must've seen it in her face, heard it in her voice. He stared at her, trying to devise a motive or weighing the possibility of getting out of this alive from her expression, but she didn't have anything left to give. He had no reason to follow through. In fact, he had every reason to walk right back to his position at the door, but he didn't. The guard rounded behind her.

In a frenzy of doubt and uncertainty, Elena closed her eyes. The sound of a blade skimming against leather—something she'd grown all too familiar with in her marriage—pricked at her nerves. Right before the ropes fell from around her wrists. Blood rushed back into her hands.

"I'll stall them as much as I can. Tell Ivy something for me." He kept his voice so low, she wasn't sure if she'd heard him right. "Tell her Echo got off his leash."

"What?" What the hell was happening? She'd asked him to release her hands. Now he was helping her? She felt the need to turn around, but every second she tried getting answers was a lost opportunity to escape. "You know Ivy?"

"You don't have much time." He shoved to his feet behind her, a serrated blade inches from her face. The guard pulled back his shoulders and watched the door as though preparing for an oncoming fight. "Metias keeps the new recruits on the second floor on the south side of the building. Your brother should be there. But I need you to do something first. You have to stab me."

"You're out of your mind." Elena got to her feet. "If Metias comes back and it doesn't look like I tried to keep you here, he will kill me, and years of undercover work will be for nothing." He took a step into her, handing her the blade handle-first. "Just imagine I'm your husband. Should make it easier. And make sure to take the knife with you. You're going to need it."

"Ex-husband." Elena sucked in a deep breath. She'd never stabbed someone before, and her gut soured at the idea. Trying to get her balance, she shifted her weight between both feet. The knife felt too heavy in her hand. She was going to have to do this. Trust him. "Any preferences on location?"

"Right here. Not too deep." He tapped just below his right pectoral. "My liver will grow back someday."

"Just promise me you're not going to die." Was she actually considering this?

"We're all dying, Elena. It's just a matter of when and what we do with the time we have left," he said.

That was too philosophical in a moment where a stranger she'd believed to be a cartel member was asking her to stab him. "Who are you?"

"You're out of time." He notched his chin higher. "Metias will be back any minute. Stab me, then get to your brother. Now."

Elena pressed the tip of the blade into the spot he'd indicated and glanced up to gauge his reaction. "Thank you."

She pushed the blade through T-shirt and flesh.

His groan would stay with her for the rest of her life, but even worse, the sound his body made as she withdrew the weapon. Blood coated the once flawless steel. She'd thought the knife was heavy before. Only now it would weigh on her from this moment forward. "I'm so sorry."

He dropped to the floor, doubling over, and she backed away. "Tell…Ivy what I said. Go!"

Elena lunged for the door, clothing clinging to her from the water drenching her down to bone. She ripped it open without looking back and pumped her

legs as fast as possible. Bunker-like lights flickered
as she raced along the corridor. *Second floor. Second
floor.* How did she get to the second floor?

Low voices echoed down the hall, and she pressed
herself against one wall. Out of breath, she tried to
keep her heart rate under control, but it was no use.
She'd just stabbed a man at his request. *Echo got off
his leash. Echo got off his leash.*

The voices had drifted farther away now. She took a
single step toward an upcoming corner, blade pressed
against her chest in defense, and rounded into a per-
pendicular corridor.

Confronting the man who'd sworn to have her in
sickness…and in death.

SHE HAD TO be here.

Cash blinked to keep himself conscious, but he was
losing the battle faster than he expected. He couldn't
recall the turns he'd already taken or how long ago
Tiny had finally collapsed. There were too many hall-
ways, and he was on his own, but he wouldn't stop.
Not until he put Bear and Elena in his sights.

His shoulder made contact with the nearest wall.
He took a second to clear his head, but the only image
his brain could come up with was of Elena. Of her
passed out in the back of his SUV, then the horror
on her face as he told her she'd mistaken Bear's allergy meds for an Oreo. Of her smile and the way it'd
tunneled past his guard as he'd invited her into his

personal space. A space he hadn't let anyone else—
not even his team—step foot in.

Hell, she'd taken on a fight no one had ever won.
Just imagining the trouble she was giving her ex and
the soldiers in this very building was enough to make
him shove away from the wall and keep going. Elena
Navarro was everything he'd tried avoiding over the
past year and the one person who could drive him to
keep going. She challenged him in ways that messed
with his head but strengthened his moral code. The
kind of woman who protected those she cared about,
who stood alone against an army determined to tear
her to pieces for the chance to do the right thing.
Who carried everyone around her with her strength.
Because that was how she quietly survived. That
was how she kept moving forward. And he needed
a healthy dose of that strength now.

Pain arced through his back as he pushed along
the corridor. His right leg dragged behind him. He
was getting close. He could feel it, and with two more
turns through the maze, he froze.

Barking.

Incessant. Distant. Undeniably familiar. Bear.

"I'm coming, little lady. Keep it up." Cash picked
up the pace. For as much pressure squeezed the oxygen from his lungs at the thought of putting off finding Elena, he wasn't going anywhere without his dog.
Bear had been there. Suffered at his side after the
explosion that got her kicked out of the DEA. Even

temporarily blind and through the painful nights following her injury, she'd refused to leave his side. Because she'd known. She'd known his loss. She'd felt
it herself when they'd recovered Wade's body miles
from the raid site where he'd died. The Colombian
cartel had done a good job of making his brother unrecognizable, but he and Bear had known the moment
they'd seen him. The whine of a K-9 that'd lost her
handler would stay with him for the rest of his life.
He wouldn't put her through that again. He wasn't
walking away.

An alarm sounded overhead.

Piercing agony ripped through his head in a swirl
of red lights and sirens.

Covering his ears, he made out heavy footfalls
coming down the corridor. Cash took a sharp right
turn to get out of their path, his back against the wall.
A group of armed men sprinted in two straight lines
down the hall, hustling as though the building were
about to collapse.

Someone could've found the mess he'd left behind
and raised the alarm, or… "Elena."

He was searching on borrowed time. They had to
get out of here. Cash couldn't hear Bear's warnings
over the sound of the alarm, but she was close. He
kept low and moved fast past a handful of doors, instincts on high alert for another swarm of soldiers.
Then he heard it. A single bark. Pulling up short,

he backed up, pressing his ear to the last door in the hall. There it was again. "Got you."

He didn't know what waited for him on the other side of the door. Didn't care. Ripping the door open, Cash rushed the armed gunman pointing a weapon at his dog as the soldier turned to confront the intruder. He cocked his elbow back and rocketed his fist into the guy's face.

The soldier dropped harder than a bag of cement, and Cash collected the man's automatic rifle as a reward. Bear cocked her head from behind a chain-link kennel, as though she'd been waiting for him all this time. "Don't give me that look. I got here as soon as I could."

He unlocked the hatch keeping her inside and crouched. Threading his fingers into her soft coat, he checked her over for injuries. Relief washed over him as he set his forehead against hers. "Good to see you, too."

Teeth bared, she stared down the soldier who'd threatened her with coal-black eyes. "Don't mind him. He's not getting up for a while. Think you can find Elena?"

With a lick of one side of her mouth, Bear hustled out the door and into the hallway. After a split second of consideration, she charged right at full speed.

He struggled to keep up with her, biting the inside of his mouth between his molars to take his brain's attention off the pain. The alert had been going for several minutes. The entire building was about to go under lockdown. No one in or out. Bear took a sharp left up ahead, out of sight. Tucking the rifle against his chest, Cash put any adrenaline still lingering in his veins into catching up.

He slowed at the corner, cutting his gaze the length of the corridor. Bear was there. Circling some kind of puddle on the floor. Heel-toeing it against the far wall, he cleared the hall. "What you got, girl? What is it?"

Bear lay down beside the stain. One of her cues to indicate human remains.

Blood. An entire foot-span seeped into the concrete. Fresh. No crusting around the edges where there was less volume. "Where is she?"

Bear's whine bled through the resounding peal of the alarm. His gut filled in the answer to his own question, but he wanted to outright reject it. No. Whoever'd lost this much blood would be well on their way to bleeding out, but it wasn't Elena. He hadn't failed her. He hadn't walked her straight to her death. She was alive. He had to believe that. Because if she wasn't… If she wasn't, then what the hell good was he?

Drops spattered out from the puddle left behind, and Cash couldn't help but follow. *"Such."* Track.

They moved as a team, Bear at his side. Shadows darkened in corners with each flash of the emergency lighting. He hiked the butt of the rifle into his shoulder and followed the trail. Elena would be at the end. There was no other option. Not for him.

The slam of something heavy ricocheted through him. Cash spun, finger on the trigger, in time to catch a barrier wall lowering down, cutting off his escape from behind. The building had gone into lockdown. Windows, doors, the garage. They wouldn't be able to get through any of it. *"Geh rein!"* Go!

Bear launched forward as a steel door started dropping four feet ahead of them. She cleared the door in record time, but his leg had gone numb. Limping didn't do a damn bit of good. The door would secure in five seconds or less. He had to move. Now. Sliding the rifle underneath, Cash lunged. His shoulder took the brunt of the impact as he rolled. The steel lock pin caught on his shirt, tearing through the thin fabric, but he'd made it.

Just in time to watch the third door seal them inside the corridor. Hell. They'd been cut off. The alarm cut out. The lights returned to normal. The threat had been neutralized. Cash listened for movement on either side of the steel barriers. There was no way through these doors without heavy machinery. No way to get to Elena.

Bear's barking echoed off the walls, then quieted as the crackle of a PA system filled the resulting silence. Cash collected the rifle he'd taken off the unconscious soldier back in the kennel and checked the rounds left in the magazine. Full load.

"You've made quite a mess, Mr. Meyers." The voice. He'd heard it before. In the dark. It was smooth, the kind that could just as easily start a war as it could declare world peace. Elena's ex. The cartel lieutenant responsible for the destruction of an entire town and the kidnapping of an eight-year-old boy. "Yes, I know who you are. Just as I know you triggered an SOS signal to the rest of your team. Unfortunately for you, they never received it. I did find something you lost though."

A struggle sounded over the intercom. Heavy breathing. "Cash, go! Get out while you still can!" Her voice muffled as though someone had shoved a gag in her mouth.

Elena. The muscles down his spine hardened one by one. It didn't matter that he couldn't see through one eye or that his leg might never recover. He'd shoot as many cartel soldiers as it took to get to her. "You son of a bitch. I warned you what would happen if you touched her. I'm going to find you, and when I do, you're going to wish you'd listened."

A bright laugh cackled through the system. "You know what, Mr. Meyers, I like you. Come." The door to his right retracted back into the ceiling from whence it'd come. "Let us do this man-to-man as in the old days. Two men fighting to win the fair maiden's heart."

The blood spatter trailed along the corridor. What would he find at the end? Not a fair fight. That much was clear. Cash positioned the rifle's stock into his shoulder and took aim, Bear on high alert. Another door retracted, leading him through the maze in turn. Until the last revealed the group of soldiers waiting on the other side.

The lieutenant—a man close to his midforties—took position in the middle, his white suit stark against the backdrop of cement and fluorescent light. With Elena restrained over his left shoulder. "Ah, yes. The man who took down five soldiers with nothing but a dumbbell and his own strength. I'm glad to see the dog survived. I'm an animal lover myself."

Cash tracked the bloodstains into the mass of men pointing guns back at him and locked his gaze on Elena. Red stained the cuff of one of her shirt sleeves, and his heart double-timed it into his throat. "You good, Elle?"

She dropped that bloody cuff away from her midsection, exposing the tip of what looked like a serrated blade in her palm. Tucked beneath her clothing. Not her blood. "Yeah. I'm good."

Chapter Nine

He'd come for her.

She wasn't sure why that was such a surprise other than the fact that no one other than her parents had dared cross Metias. They'd tried to get to her, spotting the signs she'd married a monster from a mile away, but her husband had isolated her well. It was only after she'd come to terms with her failing marriage that she realized she had to be the one to take that first step. That she needed to be brave.

And she'd do it again. Not just for herself this time. For Cash.

The tip of the blade pricked her palm. Surrounded by Metias's men, she wasn't sure how they were going to get themselves out of this, but she trusted the man who'd saved her from a cartel abduction once before. Elena rotated her forearm toward her body to conceal the weapon. It was still stained with the guard's blood. Now it would save her and Cash's lives.

"Here's what's going to happen, Mr. Meyers. You

and your dog have done enough damage, so I'm going to give you the chance to walk away." Only Metias didn't negotiate. It was a lie. There was no way her ex would let Cash or Bear survive after what they'd done.

"Just like that?" Interest sparked in Cash's voice, but an underlying suspicion narrowed his gaze. He was too intelligent to believe a word out of a warlord's mouth. "And Elena? Her brother? What happens to them?"

"They'll stay here. Of course." Metias glanced back over his shoulder to the men behind him, a scoff escaping that perfect mouth. "Where they belong."

"In that case." Cash cut his attention to her, and in that moment, she knew. She knew what he was about to do, and he was relying on her to do her part. It was the only way they were going to get out of here alive. "No deal."

In her next breath, she gathered every ounce of courage she could hold on to. "Metias." She waited for her ex to turn toward her. "This is for locking me in that cellar."

Elena let the blade drop from inside her shirt sleeve and grabbed the handle before the knife hit the cement. She stabbed the blade into the side of his thigh. His scream pierced her eardrums as she lunged to escape the ring of his security detail.

One caught her around the waist. A bullet threw his head back, and the soldier hit the floor. Bear growled from somewhere behind her. She wasn't sure, but she couldn't slow down enough to try to keep track of her and her handler. The second floor. This was her only chance to find Daniel.

A rain of gunfire ricocheted off the wall to her left. Cut off by a deep grunt and a bellowing howl. Covering her head as though her hands could stop bullets, she wrenched free of the circle of remaining guards. Oxygen caught in her chest as a strong hand threaded between her rib cage and arm.

"I've got you." Cash had to feel her shaking. It'd be impossible to miss, but they were still in the middle of a *Sangre por Sangre* complex with no way out but up. "Don't stop. Keep moving."

The shaking was getting worse. She tried to take a full breath but was on the brink of losing any control she'd somehow held on to.

"After them!" Metias's voice barreled through her and kick-started something in her brain. If she stopped to get herself together, she and Cash would die.

The outline of a soldier materialized ahead.

Cash didn't hesitate. He raised the automatic rifle slung around his chest and fired. The threat didn't stand a chance against the hail of gunfire and collapsed. Bear's claws scratched along the cement as loud as a typewriter. "Are you hurt?"

"No. It's… It's not my blood." The feel of the blade penetrating the flesh and organ of that guard was still fresh. Elena wiped her hands down the front of her jeans to drown the memory, but it was no use. She'd stabbed a man. Not including her ex-husband. And now she was carrying his blood with her. "Second floor... We have to get t-to the second floor." She caught herself against the wall as they reached the end of the maze. Stairs vibrated under their ascent. "Daniel's there."

Cash took aim up the boxy windup of steel stairs as though he'd done it a thousand times before. Anyone looking down would instantly see them, but he kept moving up, focused and routined. Hesitating at the first landing, he leaned to one side to get a better view before charging up to the next platform. A low growl seemed to enunciate his every step.

A spatter of bullets exploded from above.

Bear knocked into her shin, and Elena made contact with the wall. Out of the way. Cash twisted around, exposing the swelling and blood marring his handsome face. She'd seen it before but had underestimated the damage. He wouldn't be able to see out of his left eye, yet as he squeezed the rifle's trigger, every round found its mark. He latched onto her wrist and pulled her after him, and the raw skin there burned at his touch.

Her ears were ringing. Her hands were shaking. They stepped over the two soldiers who'd tried to kill them. One grabbed for her ankle, but Bear ensured his release with a snap of teeth and warning.

"This is it." Cash hugged the gun to his chest,

barrel pointed down as he surveilled what waited for them on the other side of the heavy door with nothing but a rectangle of two-paned glass. "How do you know Daniel's here?"

"One of the guards. He told me this is where Metias keeps the new recruits. He was…trying to help me." But could she trust he'd given her good information? Was she supposed to believe he wasn't really *Sangre por Sangre* but an impostor? A plant to mine the cartel for intel? *Tell Ivy Echo got off his leash.* Her gut said yes, but it'd lied to her in the past. About Metias. About her ability to keep her family safe. About her choice to collect information about the cartel. She'd been wrong. About everything. "He let me go. He was helping me."

She was rambling now. Trying to justify her reasons for wanting to stay when every other thought in her brain was telling her they needed to get the hell out of here, that Cash needed a doctor or an entire emergency medical team. But she couldn't go. Not without Daniel.

Cash centered himself in her vision, and it took everything she had left to keep him there. The tremors raced up her arms. Made her cold. She wanted to reach out for him, needed that contact to keep her standing. He angled the gun down and behind his back on its lanyard and gripped both of her arms as though sensing exactly what was happening. "Easy.

Breathe. Look at me. We're not leaving here until we search the floor. Okay? So let's find him."

She nodded. It was easier to breathe with his hands on her right then. The invisible connection they'd both somehow entered into over the past two days steadied her more than ever before, and she had no doubt in her mind she was only alive because of a stranger and his dog. "Okay."

Cash shifted the rifle back into his hands, and they went through the door. It was quiet. Darker than the basement without overhead lights. A set of rare windows in a compound meant to be buried allowed a wash of sunlight through the open room but it didn't carry far with a layer of tint. Fifty or more empty cots—disheveled and slept-in—peppered the entirety of the floor.

"I don't… I don't understand." Elena pressed her hand into one cot. The once-white sheet was cold. An indent in the center of the pillow told her someone had been there. The information the guard had given her wasn't wrong. But whoever'd slept there had been gone awhile. Same with the rest. "Where are the recruits? Where are the guards?"

She moved through the sterile room, searching each cot for something—anything—to confirm Daniel had been there or where he might've gone. The soldiers they'd encountered had all been men. Not boys. Metias had them moved. He'd known exactly why she'd come, and he'd done what he could to make sure she'd fail. To punish her. His offer to let Daniel go had been a lie. Even if she'd agreed to come back to him, he never would've let her see her brother again.

Frustration and a toxic dose of grief pressurized behind her sternum. She'd survived three days in a cellar, a cartel raid and house fire, an abduction and getting shot at. But this… This would be what broke her. Anger pushed tears into her eyes. "He's not here."

Cash scanned the room. A low rumble of voices infiltrated the silence. He headed for the nearest window. "We have to go."

It wasn't supposed to be like this. Bear nudged at her legs from behind, urging her to follow Cash, and Elena's body complied, but her mind? It was someplace else altogether. On the black, red and gold dragon-unicorn she'd gotten for her brother for Valentine's Day last year. The one he'd dropped during their escape from the house. She should've gone back for it as he'd asked. She should've given him something to hold on to when he'd gotten scared and wondered if anyone was looking for him.

She failed to process Cash's commands. He turned to her, shouting something she couldn't hear over the ringing in her head. The window shattered under the strength of his bullets, and a burst of descending sun beamed into her face. She brought her hand up to block the onslaught. Everything seemed to play out in slow motion. Cash hauling one leg over the windowsill. Bear hopping up on her hind legs.

Even the door slamming open behind them.

A flood of soldiers swarmed inside, though they were still too far away and slowed down by the layout of cots to reach them. What was the point? Without her brother, why bother escaping at all? The answer solidified in front of her as Cash took her hand and tugged her after him into the sunlight.

Because without her, Daniel didn't have a chance at all.

HE ALMOST HADN'T made it.

"You're lucky to be alive." The doc beamed a flashlight straight into his eyes, and a whole new kind of pain ignited through his head. "Tell me what happened."

"I started swinging. A few guys might've gotten in the way." He'd blacked out on the way back to headquarters. If it hadn't been for Elena taking the wheel, *Sangre por Sangre* would've been on them. It wouldn't take long before the cartel struck back. That was how it worked out here in the desert. An eye for an eye. Blood for blood. And from what he'd gauged from that lieutenant, this had become more than a territory war. This was personal.

"Right. I'm betting they look a lot worse." The dark blue scrubs and dark cardigan only added to Dr. Nafessa Piel's allure. Black hair framed a slim face and accentuated sepia, reddish-brown skin. In truth, Cash didn't know a whole lot about her.

As Socorro's one and only doctor on call, she took doctor-patient confidentiality to a whole new level. She didn't let anything slip. "Headache? Nausea? Vomiting? Dizziness? Any fogginess?"

"Is it bad if I say all of the above?" He'd known there was a possibility of a concussion considering the beating he'd taken before returning the favor to the group of soldiers in the gym. And the way his brain was rattling around in his head like it had after the explosion from his brother's DEA raid was a pretty good sign that something wasn't right. "The woman I brought in. Elena. Where is she?"

The flashlight was gone now. In its place, the doc pressed a cold stethoscope to his back and pulled his shoulder back. "I cleared her while Jones and Granger were pulling you out of the car. No serious injuries. Breathe in for me."

Seeing as how Elena had cleared her physical and Dr. Piel held the future of his assignments in her thin hands, he did as he was told.

"I don't hear any fluid in your lungs, but you're going to have to take it easy on that rib. As for the leg, nothing broken as far as I can tell. The X-rays should be back in a couple of days to confirm it, but you're most likely looking at a dislocated knee joint. Once the swelling goes down, I'll be able to reset it." She moved around the room, discarding her latex gloves in the trash and grabbing up her tablet and stylus to take notes. "Until then, get some rest, take an ice bath, elevate that knee and keep a compression sleeve around it. Should be good as new for you to mess up within a couple weeks."

He shifted his weight onto his good leg as he dropped off the exam table. "Don't know what I'd do without you, Doc."

"Probably die." She didn't even bother looking up from her notes as she said it. "All of you operatives think you're invincible. I just hope I'm there when you realize you're not."

True enough. The men and women of Socorro had seen their share of pain and violence and scars. It was what made them the elite—the right choice in fighting an enemy who didn't play by the rules. Each member of the team knew the stakes and the devastation that could follow if they didn't take risks. And sometimes that included believing they were invincible from time to time.

His leg bummed out on him halfway to his room. The brace Doc Piel had strapped around his knee helped with stability, but his endurance had gone to hell. She'd insisted on putting Bear in the kennel for the night instead of his room to give him a chance at some solid sleep, but the memories were right there at the front of his mind. They weren't going to give him the chance. Every mistake he'd made. Every hit he'd taken. Every drop of blood he'd lost.

"Damn. What house dropped on you today? Jones just told me he had to drag you out of the garage."

Jocelyn slowed her approach, every thought splayed across her face as usual. Right now her expression was broadcasting concern. Like a mom who'd just found out her kid had gotten into a fight at school. "Your face is a mess."

"Good to see you, too, Joce," he said.

She gripped his head between both hands and prodded at the butterfly stitch at the corner of his eye. "You should've called me. I'd have been there to back you up."

"I did." He didn't like this. The boundaries she insisted on breaking in an effort to bring the team closer together. The movie nights, the birthday parties, the dinners together at the table. None of it made up for what they'd each lost. Pretending it would only made things worse. They weren't a family. Hell, they weren't even friends most of the time. They were a highly-skilled operations unit. Yeah, they trusted one another. They had each other's backs when the time came, but this personal stuff? He didn't want any part of it. Didn't need it.

Except when the going had gotten tough back in that compound, there'd only been one person on his mind. Elena. It would've taken a massive amount of courage to confront her ex like that, let alone stab the man. He thought back to what the doc had said. Elena hadn't suffered any serious injuries, but the blood on her sleeve had been fresh. Cash maneuvered past

Jocelyn, leg be damned. "Cartel must've killed the signal. Nothing was getting through."

"Don't wait so long next time," she said. "And eat some vegetables. Not that garbage you call a cookie."

Because there would be a next time. The entire team was on alert. Waiting for the cartel to regroup and strike. It was only a matter of time, but tonight... He didn't have to worry about tonight. Cash hobbled down the hall and shoved into his room. She was there, sitting at the edge of his bed as though waiting for him all this time.

She pushed to her feet as he closed the door behind him. Not a word.

"Hey." He didn't know what else to say. Honestly, there wasn't anything he could say. They'd barely survived the search for her brother and come back empty-handed. She'd risked her life and her mental health, knowing what waited for her on the inside of that building, to bring her brother home. And she'd failed. A rock-bottom pit he was all too used to staring up from. "You hungry?"

Elena crossed the distance between them. She slammed into his chest, securing her arms around him so tight he felt as though she'd crack another of his ribs. Only Cash didn't care. She angled her ear over his heart, and a sense of calm he'd only felt when Bear climbed into his bed at night took over. "I'm sorry."

"Don't." He threaded one hand into the hair along

her nape, urging her to look up at him. She locked near-black eyes on him, so intense he could've sworn he saw himself in the reflection of her irises. Deep purple and blue bruises bloomed along one cheek, and a wave of rage crested at the sight. "What happened back there wasn't your fault. None of it. You understand me? I knew what I was getting myself into when I agreed to help you find him, and there was nothing you could've done differently."

She pressed one hand against his chest. "How bad is it?"

"I won't be running a marathon anytime soon, but seeing as how I wasn't interested in killing myself for a medal to hang on my wall before, I think I'll survive." He released his hold in her hair, loving the way it felt between his fingers. How it caught on the calluses, then slid free. It was slightly damp. She'd showered, and it was then he realized she'd changed. His oversize shirt and sweatpants did nothing to hide the woman underneath, and Cash couldn't help but appreciate her style.

Her smile cracked despite the tension moving in on the corners of her mouth. She slipped her hand from his chest, taking a bit of warmth with her. "You always know just what to say. Has your team learned anything more since we escaped the compound?"

He knew what she was asking, but he didn't have any answers for her. "Satellite images recorded a blizzard of activity in the minutes after we broke into the compound. From the look of it, six soldiers were moving a group of people out of the building into a truck on the other side."

She seemed to steel herself for the conclusion. "Daniel?"

"That's what it looks like," he said. "Metias must've ordered the evacuation after he ambushed us in the corridor. Since then construction has been halted, and the fleet of vehicles we suspected on site was deployed."

"Looking for us." It wasn't a question. They both knew what was coming. All they could do was prepare for what happened next.

He nodded. "They followed the SUV's tire tracks up until about a mile out. Guess they were hoping we'd have car trouble. Catch us out in the open. Would have, too, if it weren't for you behind the wheel."

"You make it sound like I wasn't the one who almost got you killed." Elena hugged herself then, goose bumps traveling up her arms. She was holding herself together as though expecting to shatter into a million pieces right there in the middle of the floor. The adrenaline, the fear—it drained fast and left the body in shock if you weren't prepared for it. "Thank you. For coming for me. I wasn't sure…"

Cash countered the space she'd added between them. "If I'd hold up my end of the deal. I would've done the same in your position. Trusting someone with your life like that. It feels…wrong sometimes. We tell ourselves we're strong enough, that we are all we need, when it comes right down to it. But in the end, we really don't want to be alone."

"No. We don't." A softness transformed her expression as she looked up at him, and Elena took that last step separating them. "Cash, I know Ivy arranged a room for me to stay in tonight, but...could I please stay here? With you? Because I really don't want to be alone."

He didn't have to think his answer through. "Yeah. You can take the bed. I'll sleep on the couch. That's usually where Bear passes out, but she's in the kennel tonight. Though I've gotta warn you—I might wake up smelling like dog in the morning."

"No." She skimmed her fingers down his forearm and interlaced her fingers with his. She tugged him forward despite the differences in their sizes. "Not on the couch."

Chapter Ten

The swelling had gone down in his face.

Elena pressed her head into the pillow as sunrise broke over the mountains from the east. It cast across the bridge of his nose and highlighted the damage done less than twelve hours ago.

He was still asleep. All dark bruises, lacerations and intensity, even unconscious. Cash had done as she asked. He'd stayed with her. Held her. For the first time in the past three days, she'd let herself unravel, and he'd been there to hold her together.

But she could still feel a thin coat of blood on her hands. The guard's. Metias's. She'd scrubbed her skin raw during her shower last night, but it wouldn't come off. She wasn't sure it ever would. Holding a man's life in her hands had all at once been powerful and terrifying. Metias had deserved what she'd done, but she couldn't help but wonder what became of the operative who'd helped her escape.

Silence secured her in a vulnerable blanket of unease. She'd been running on fumes for so long, it felt wrong to stay here in bed, memorizing Cash's face. Every angle, the cleft in his chin, the scar cutting through his eyebrow. All of it puzzled together to create a work of art. And she appreciated art. She wanted to remember this moment. The one encapsulating two people who'd been through hell and survived. Together.

"You're supposed to be asleep." His voice seemed to stick to the edges of his throat.

"I've never been a great sleeper." Elena buried deeper under the comforter they shared. Despite living with a Rottweiler, Cash had managed to keep the bed hair- and odor-free. Instead, there was a hint of the bodywash she'd found in the shower last night. Something clean and masculine. Something specific to the man beside her. She breathed it in a bit deeper.

He twisted with a grimace of pain in his expression to read the alarm clock on the nightstand over her shoulder, bringing him closer. "How long have you been up?"

"Long enough to notice your tattoo." She hadn't believed what she'd seen at first. This ex-military operator had gotten a tattoo on his hip of a muffin with bulging biceps, a tattooed anchor on one arm and a banner wrapping the entire piece of artwork. "Stud muffin."

His laughter punctured through the room and wedged under her rib cage to break apart the vise around her lungs. Cash scrubbed a hand down his face. He smiled then, stretching the split in his lip, but he didn't show any signs of noticing. "Right. I could tell you I don't remember getting it or that my marine buddies played a prank on me, but the truth is, my brother's is much worse."

"You and your brother got tattoos together?" She could imagine it. A younger version of the soldier in front of her and a DEA analyst making an undeniable pact to go through a unique kind of pain together. Judging by the lift of his mouth, it was a memory Cash obviously cherished. Even after everything that'd happened between them, he would still have that. He still remembered the good times. Could she say the same if she lost Daniel?

"Day we enlisted." He shook his head, flexing the muscles and tendons along his bare shoulders. While they hadn't done more than hold each other through the night, the temptation to test that strength for herself was there. Just beneath the surface. "Crazy, I know, but it made sense at the time."

"No. I think it's sweet." She tugged the comforter down, exposing the tattoo, and traced a line around the muffin's top. "The two of you taking on the world together with matching hip tattoos."

"Wade's is a pink doughnut with sprinkles," he said.

Secondhand embarrassment pooled in her stomach. "Oh, no."

He hiked himself onto his elbow, as though nothing outside of this room mattered. And it felt good. While she'd initially feared what being the center of this man's attention would result in, she found there wasn't anywhere else she'd rather be right then. "It says 'I'm a-dough-rable' in cursive."

"That's terrible." She wanted to cringe and laugh at the same time. "But I would've loved to have seen it." The words were already out of her mouth before she realized her mistake. "Cash, I'm sorry. I didn't mean—"

"Don't worry about it. What's done is done. Wade made his choice, and he paid for it. Nothing anyone can do about it now." The smile was gone then. "That tattoo was the only way to identify his body. Cartel dumped him in the middle of the desert."

"You went back for him." Of course he had. Because that was the kind of man Cash Meyers was. The kind that trusted little but once he did, he went the added mile. Who suffered betrayal and loss and heartache but ensured justice for those he cared for. Who kept his word to a woman who'd nearly gotten him killed. He was rational and ethical and kind, and once he started a mission, he finished it. No matter the cost. He didn't hold grudges. He fought for the weak and put others first. He was the opposite of her ex in every way, shape and form, and her heart beat harder at the thought of being one of the people he fought for.

Elena shifted closer, framing her hand along his jaw. Her thumb found the butterfly bandage at the far side of his left eye and smoothed the edges. His exhale brushed along her neck as he set dark eyes on her. He could feel it, too. That need to get close, to rely on someone other than himself. Metias had stolen that and her ability to forge relationships from her, but he couldn't touch this. Not if she didn't let him.

She kept her gaze locked on him as she pressed her mouth to his.

It was probably the most inappropriate thing to do to a man who'd just told her how he'd been able to identify his brother's body, but Cash seemed to accept this for what it was. Pure need. Fire licked up her insides the moment he penetrated the seam of her lips. His hand found the sensitive spot at her lower back and hauled her into his body. He was strong, stronger than any man she'd ever known, and she needed that strength. He held on to her as though he might break if he let go. Like she mattered.

This was insanity. People weren't supposed to meet like this. In the middle of a war between a brutal cartel and the small towns they were trying to take over. Maybe if she'd had a normal life—one without Metias, without the threat of losing her brother, without not knowing if her parents were all right— they could've met someplace else. He'd still brood, and she'd like that about him. They'd flirt, and she'd laugh at his sarcasm. They'd go on a date and make plans to do it again.

Instead, they were here. In a dorm-like room with an empty dog bed shoved against the wall and the sun coming up over the mountain. Each seeking something only found in the other, and Elena poured everything into finding what she needed. Protection, safety. Control. Somehow since the night of the raid, Cash had pulled her free of sinking into an endless well of loss she wasn't sure she would ever escape. Loss of the life she'd imagined, of her family, of any semblance of the woman she thought she knew.

Now there was something bright to hold on to. She and Cash knew grief and betrayal. They knew loneliness. What if they could create something new? What if they could forget the violence and bloodshed outside of these walls and just be? What she wouldn't give to be able to do that for him, to help him escape his pain as he'd done for her.

His heartbeat raged against her hand as he urged her calf around his thigh, inching them closer in every regard. This wasn't a biological reaction to danger that drove her. This was something more. Something real. And it was everything.

She'd hidden away from this, left the ability to trust and feel behind in Albuquerque. She'd had to. To survive. To protect herself. Afraid it would slither back into her heart and finish her off for good. But Cash had barreled through her every intention to keep him at a distance, and she ached at the thought of what she'd missed by shutting everyone out. At what could've happened if she'd just said yes to Deputy McCrae for dinner or if she'd been able to live with a husband who kept secrets. Deep down though, she knew. It was Cash. No one else would do. Because none of them were him.

The tick of something quick and heavy grew louder, pulling Elena from the drugging kiss.

Cash ducked his chin. "Oh, no. Prepare yourself."

"For what?" Her question went unanswered.

Until Bear bounded through the dog door, tongue flying, eyes alive. She launched her entire frame up onto the bed and padded between Elena and Cash in tight circles. The dog's tail hit Elena in the side of the face with enough force to knock her back onto her pillow. Playful growls vibrated through Bear.

"I know, girl. I know. I missed you, too." Cash propped himself up in bed, the comforter sliding down to reveal a perfectly outlined set of ab muscles that Elena had been so close to testing for herself. He scratched at Bear's neck and ruffled her coat. "You couldn't just give me a few more minutes though?"

It was endearing and cute, the way Cash and Bear loved each other, and the view of them reunited stuck in her throat. What she'd felt before had seemed real in the moment, but her heart hurt now. Watching

them, seeing how happy they made each other...
She didn't fit. Just as she hadn't fit in her marriage.
She was a nobody to them. An assignment. She'd
shoved her way into their lives because she wanted
her brother back. Helping her was a job, and one kiss
wasn't going to change that. And she'd been a fool
to believe it could mean more. She tried to breathe
around the ache inside but couldn't seem to fill her
lungs. "Excuse me."

"Everything okay?" he asked.

"Fine." Elena didn't let herself slow down as she
swung her feet to the floor and rounded the bed toward the bathroom. She closed the bathroom door
behind her and secured the lock. Twisting the shower
handle to the hottest position, she swiped at the tears
and unpocketed the phone she'd kept hidden from
Cash.

Her darkest shame rose as she read through the
message inbox.

Happily-ever-after didn't exist. At least not for her.

ELENA DIDN'T TASTE anything like dog allergy medicine.

There'd been mint from the toothpaste in the bathroom and a sweetness to counter it he couldn't de-
scribe. She'd been soft and hard all at the same time,
hesitant and demanding, stripped of that emotional
armor she wore yet raw for him.

Mere seconds with her had alleviated hours of
pain, frustration and doubt of this assignment, and

he wanted nothing more than to escape back into that cocoon they'd built around themselves the past few hours. Because inside it—with her—he'd felt like himself for the first time in over a year. Not the whatever-it-takes contractor he'd become, but the man who'd jumped at the opportunity to work alongside his brother and the DEA. The one who'd known where his path would take him since the day he'd enlisted in the military and was up for the challenge of making the world a little bit safer.

He'd lost sight of that side of him after his brother's death. Something inside of him had gone cold. Empty. He'd felt it, like a void continuously shifting and growing in his chest. It didn't matter how many assignments he and Bear had taken on or what the job was. Nothing had come close to healing that hollowness.

Until last night. As he'd held Elena. Inhaled the sharpness of her shampoo and conditioner, slid his hands along her skin. He'd enjoyed his fair share of women throughout the years. Some he'd met through Wade, others in a nearby bar. Always temporary. Yeah, he thought he'd been in love as a kid with his high school girlfriend before they'd figured out they were on separate trajectories, but last night… Something had changed.

Something inside him had trusted her enough to tell her about Wade when he hadn't mentioned him to another living soul other than the DEA higher-ups and his commanding officer after their operation blew up in his face. Elena wasn't like the others. She didn't conform to what she thought he might want to hear or try to be someone who hadn't been through some terrible stuff. She was honest. She was good. And she made him want to leave the past in the past. To move forward. To take the good when it came.

But Elena hadn't said a word since they'd left Socorro headquarters. Didn't even seem to notice him as she studied the open landscape through the windshield.

They'd agreed to warn Alpine Valley of the potential for another raid from the cartel. Her friend, the deputy, had come back clean. No outlandish debt other than the mortgage on his small home. No payments into his accounts other than from the city. Not even a speeding ticket. Cartels like *Sangre por Sangre* liked to use small-town police forces to keep an eye out. Departments were plugged in to their communities, trusted in most cases and able to gather intel under the banner of public safety. Deputy McCrae's background check didn't highlight any of the telltale signs Cash had uncovered when he'd looked into his brother's activities leading up to his death. They would trust him. For now.

The SUV's shocks absorbed the change from desert dirt to asphalt as he drove them into the town limits. The smoke had cleared, though that only exposed the damage done. The small church that'd held the weight of its ancient bell off to their right—barely able to contain fifty people during mass—had collapsed in on its scalded and blackened frame. The art gallery had somehow managed to survive, though the sign on the front door had been turned to indicate they were closed. Three men of varying ages boarded the windows of the BBQ restaurant but turned to stare down their vehicle as Cash and Elena drove through. "Guess I should've brought something a little less flashy."

"They're scared." Her solemn expression reflected back from the passenger-side window. "They're wondering what comes next. How they'll rebuild. If it'll happen again. If they'll find their loved ones. They didn't have any warning."

His gut soured. The night of the raid had played back through his head so many times over the course of three days. She was right. The people of this town hadn't gotten any warning because he hadn't given them any. It'd been his responsibility to track the cartel's movements, to raise the alarm for places like this one, but he'd been too late. There was no excuse or reason he could give her for allowing the men, women and children digging through the rubble of their homes to lose what they had.

Because if he did, she'd see the truth: that he was no better than his brother who'd sentenced dozens of agents and marines to their deaths the day of the DEA raid.

Or maybe she already had.

Maybe that was why she'd added the distance between them since waking in bed together this morning.

"The station is just up ahead." She pointed through the windshield to indicate a collection of single-level buildings grouped together at the end of a cul-de-sac made up of businesses.

Wood logs placed evenly throughout a makeshift lot indicated parking spots, while a low fence divided the asphalt straight down the middle. The main building stretched the length of three trailers with red wood bannisters leading visitors and police to two separate doors. One end for court proceedings, the other for the police department. Two vehicles—a truck and a police cruiser—had backed in for an easy exit on the right end of the structure, and Cash did the same.

He shouldered out of the vehicle, scanning a small park across the road with Cat Mesa towering protectively over the village. Then he turned at the sound of the building's glass front door squeaking outward on its hinges.

The officer dressed in a black police uniform with a gold shield over his heart jogged down the stairs. A thick brown beard and mustache hid most of the man's features, but not enough for Cash to make out the concern splattered across the officer's expression. The nameplate pinned opposite his shield read *B. McCrae* in black lettering. This was the cop Elena trusted. "Elena, holy hell. When I didn't hear from you, I'd assumed the worst. Are you all right?"

McCrae didn't wait for an answer and wrapped her in a strong hug, practically lifting her off her feet. A ping of defensiveness tendriled through Cash as he caught the cop tucking his nose into Elena's hair to take a full breath. She'd said McCrae and she had been friends for years, since high school, but Cash's gut said the cop was obviously interested in something more.

She pushed herself free from McCrae's arms and took a step back. A flush of pink spread through her cheeks as she glanced toward Cash. "I'm alive, thanks to Cash and his team, but it hasn't been easy. I'll tell you everything, but I need to know my parents are okay first. Have you seen them?"

"You haven't heard?" McCrae bounced his attention between Elena and Cash, then took her hands in his. "I responded to your message. I've been trying to get a hold of you for two days to give you the news."

"Message?" Cash took position at Elena's side. They'd been careful about keeping her activity off the radar. Never staying in one place too long when they left headquarters, no phone calls, no outside communication at all. His gut tightened. The phone. The one they'd recovered from the ruins. Oh, hell.

He'd checked it for spyware, contacts and messages, but the logs had been empty. In an age where people didn't bother to memorize phone numbers with them a touch away, he hadn't considered she'd risk her life by making contact to someone in town. What had he done? "What message?"

She didn't take her eyes off McCrae. "Where are my parents?"

McCrae pulled his shoulders back, accentuating a broad chest that got attention more than a couple times a week in the gym. "They're at Lovelace Westside Hospital. Your dad… He took the brunt of what the cartel did. I don't have all the details, but I know he had to go into surgery to stop some internal bleeding. The chief is with them now. He's watching over them in case the cartel decides to finish what they started. But, Elena, I've gathered statements from everyone in town. They all say the same thing. The raid started at your house."

Elena's knees gave without warning, but Cash was right there. He caught her against his chest a split second before she turned into him. He held her as he did last night—keeping her in one piece, not missing the way McCrae seemed to gauge Cash for himself.

Bear's whine matched the turmoil cutting through him. Her ex-husband and his cartel had systematically torn Elena's life apart. Not just with abducting her brother but going after her aging parents in the same blow. Metias was isolating her all over again, taking away everything she loved, everything she had to fight for.

Psychological warfare at its worst, but the son of a bitch wouldn't win. Because she wasn't alone this time. And Cash would spend the rest of his life and every resource he had protecting her if that was what she required. "We're going to take them down, Elena. Every last one of them. They're going to pay for what they've done." ·

She added a couple inches of distance between them. "How? Their guard is up now. They're looking for us as we speak. Socorro might have the resources, but based on what we saw in that compound, we're outnumbered five times over, and I'm sure that number is higher since we escaped. And Metias won't stop. He knows I was collecting information on the cartel, and he will kill every last one of you, my parents and my brother to get it back. What you're asking… It's impossible."

Cash swiped his busted knuckles along her cheek, catching a stray tear cascading down the bruised side of her face. "Except you're not alone in this anymore. Besides, I do my best work when the odds are stacked against me."

"You really think we can stop Metias from hurting more people?" she asked.

"I told you the day I met you—I've got your back," he said. "If anything had changed, I would've let you know."

He brushed his thumb over her smile as she leaned into his palm.

McCrae raised his hand—as though they were in the middle of a classroom working out an unsolvable math problem—hesitant and awkward. "I might have a way."

Chapter Eleven

Brock McCrae led them to a small, out-of-the-way
desk once Cash had agreed to surrender his weapon
into a locker at the front of the station. Made sense.
The only guns police wanted within arm's reach were
their own in case a situation broke out. But the way
Cash kept glancing to the locker and crossing and
uncrossing his arms said he obviously didn't like it.

"Have you heard of Sensorvault?" Brock fin-
gered the scroll wheel of his computer mouse, and
his ancient, dust-covered monitor responded a few
seconds later.

Elena glanced from her friend to Cash, then back.
"Is that one of the little wizard boy books Daniel has
been reading the past couple of years?" He'd been
asking her for weeks to read them to him at night
before bed so they could have a full-blown movie
marathon together. She'd always found an excuse to
put it off. Now she wanted nothing more than to get
that chance again. To read him just a few pages of

one of his books. To tuck him in to bed. Hell, even to step on one of his LEGOs would be welcome at this point. But they'd lost everything. His toys, those books, their home.

Her stomach was still twisted at the image of Metias's men manhandling her sixty-four-year-old father. What kind of person could give that order? And why had she fallen in love with him in the first place? Elena turned her gaze toward Cash. And was she making the same mistake now?

"Not exactly." Brock's laugh shook through his office in the corner of the police department. Department was an overstatement. In Alpine Valley, the police station consisted of two double-wide trailers welded together to create some semblance of unity between the court side and the police side. Two desks, one of them belonging to the police chief and vacant at the moment, assisted the handful of officers committed to serving and protecting their small town. Dark wood paneling had been installed halfway up the wall—a half-hearted attempt to jazz the place up. Above that, gray paint peeled at the meeting place between the walls and the drop-down tile ceiling. The lights in here were something from eighties-style kitchens, but two large door-sized windows let in enough light to ensure visitors wouldn't suffer from seasonal affective disorder come winter. It was a wonder Brock and his fellow officers could do their jobs with the lack of resources on hand, but the community believed in them all the same. "Though it does tell a great story."

Bear nudged at the deputy's desk with her snout, slicking wetness all along the faux wood. There must've been some kind of food inside. Elena had known Brock to stash sweets as long as she'd known him.

"Sensorvault is a database put together by the largest internet host in existence. It collects GPS data from every phone at any given time and location and stores that information in the database only accessible by law enforcement." The words fell from Cash's mouth as though she'd simply asked him what the weather was outside. This kind of stuff was what he'd been trained for, serving in the marines and employed under a security company. This was what he was good at, and the way he maintained his focus doused the doubts circling her brain. "Geofence warrants are almost impossible to get though. You think we have a shot?"

She didn't let Brock answer. This sounded like an answer they could've used yesterday. "Wait. Are you saying we could look up anyone who was in the vicinity of where I hid the information I got on the cartel and identify who took it through their phone? Why wasn't this something you brought up earlier?"

"Socorro isn't law enforcement, and the internet host follows strict rules about who has access to their database. They are only compelled to reveal their data through a court order, and in this case, I'm not sure we have a strong enough reason to file one." Cash angled himself away from the small grouping they'd made around Brock's desk. Bear followed on his heels, always the constant companion. "Even if we did, we don't know when the phone was switched out. Hundreds of people have been up and around in those pueblos and ruins in the past few weeks alone. The host assigns the devices it tracks anonymous ID numbers. There's no way to tell who's in possession of the phone right this second without unfettered access to the database itself."

Elena had to stop herself from letting the headache at the back of her skull take over. This was why she'd wanted to go to the police the night of the raid. They could've started the process days ago instead of being forced to confront Metias head-on.

"True, but Sensorvault would narrow down the suspect list." Brock continued to scroll through what looked like a list of calls the department had responded to over the past few days. The words blurred the longer Elena tried to catch them, but he soon slowed to a stop for what he was looking for.

"You said you had a plan," she said.

"Judge Hodge was just pulled over for a DUI last week." Brock turned to them with nothing but pride on his face. "All we've got to do is get him to sign the warrant request. Election is coming up this winter. It'll work."

"Blackmail? That's your solution?" Cash scrubbed a hand down his face. A scoff rushed past his mouth as he turned from them. "What makes you think your judge is the kind of man to give in to blackmail? What's to stop him from stripping you of that badge and having you and us arrested for attempted extortion and coercion?"

Elena read through the dispatch log on McCrae's screen. *Initiated-Motor Vehicle Stop. Arrest(s) made. Driving under the influence. Deputy Brock McCrae.* The time and date stamps for arrival and clearance were all there, spanning about thirty minutes, but the log didn't identify the driver or a license plate. Still, without the information she'd collected and stored on that phone, they had no chance of tearing apart Metias's organization. They had to try.

Brock didn't seem to have an answer of his own, but Elena didn't need one. She'd already made her decision. "This is how we bring down the cartel."

"You can't be serious," Cash said.

His disapproval struck harder than she expected. Over the course of the past few days, she'd relied on him to make the right choice. Depended on his moral compass and his idealism. They were what made Cash…Cash, and they made up a big part of why she trusted him. A man so determined to prove his integrity was the extreme opposite of the one who'd isolated her from everyone she loved and what she wanted.

But Daniel was in more danger than ever since their escape last night. And following the rules hadn't gotten them anywhere close to getting him back. He had to see that. "The cartel won't stop, Cash. You don't know what it's like, living in fear all the time in a town like this. Knowing that you're not the one who gets to decide your future and just praying day in and day out that you won't be their next target. They'll keep spreading, like a plague. They'll keep corrupting everything they touch. The people here were lucky. They might not be so lucky the next time. And the information I collected could put a stop to it. We can bury Metias and kill the snake. We just need to find that phone."

"So we follow their rules, is that it?" Cash pointed a strong finger at the floor, stepping into her. "We level the playing field by becoming the exact thing we're fighting? Is this really what you want to become?"

Something tightened in her chest, but it didn't dissuade her from the option in front of them. Not when the stakes were so high. This wasn't about her or Metias or what'd happened over the past few days. This was about an eight-year-old boy who only wanted to come home to his family. "Wouldn't you if you were given the chance to save Wade?"

A hardness he'd never turned on her solidified his expression in place at the mention of his brother.

It was her turn to take a step toward him. Dragging his hand from his side, she framed it between hers. The skin along the back of his knuckles was broken and bruised, and in that moment, she saw through to the man underneath the scars and the defensiveness and sense of mission. "Brock, can you please give us a moment?"

The deputy took a loud, cleansing breath of his own, shaking his head. He shoved to his feet and locked access to his computer with a few taps of his keyboard. "Uh, yeah. Take as long as you need. I'm going to check in with the chief at the hospital."

She waited until the glass front door closed, secluding her and Cash from the rest of the world. Her thumb traced the raised edges of dead skin around his wounds. "You're not him, Cash. Your brother. What he did… There was no excuse for the damage he caused, for the trust he betrayed." Elena dropped her hold on his hand, notching her chin higher to meet his gaze. "And that's not you."

The small muscles along his jaw ticked with his racing pulse. "We were cut from the same cloth. Wade and me. We liked the same movies, talked the same way. Even dated a couple of the same girls at some point. We both knew what we had to do the moment we saw that second plane crash into the World Trade Center tower. We spent nearly every second of our lives together up until we enlisted. We didn't have the kind of relationship most siblings did. There weren't fights over who got to take the car that night or yelling about tearing a hole through a shirt of his I'd borrowed. After Dad died, we stepped up— together—to take care of Mom. Because it was the right thing to do. He was my younger brother, but I was the one who looked up to him."

Cash shifted his weight between his feet. "What if what corrupted him is in me? What if it's just waiting to claw itself out?" He had to take a breath then, his massive shoulders stiff and weighed down. "If I give in, even for something as easy as this, what's to stop me from following in his shoes? If I take that step, that's it, Elena. There's no going back, and who knows what I'll do. Or who I'll hurt."

She swallowed the constriction threatening to choke her from the inside. Taking on the pressure and the weight of his admission as her own. She had a choice. Protect Cash from himself or go after the information she'd collected to protect her brother from the cartel. Elena pressed her hand over his heart. "Okay. Then we won't go through the judge. What if we call the phone instead?"

Confusion rippled across that handsome face. "You want to call your phone to see if someone picks up?"

"No blackmail. No coloring outside the lines." She ripped a piece of paper from Brock's notepad and scratched out the number, then handed it to Cash. It was a long shot, but there was still a chance she could fix this. "One call."

"And if it doesn't work?" He picked up the phone on Brock's desk and dialed the number on an ancient LAN line that should've been put out to pasture years ago. "What then?"

She didn't have an answer.

Because a cell phone had started ringing from one of the chief's desk drawers.

"You're sure?" Cash handled the phone with a sandwich bag from Deputy McCrae's lunch to avoid compromising any prints on the device they'd recovered in the chief's desk.

"It's my phone." Elena nodded. "The dented corner on the bottom came from me dropping it on my driveway the night I ran from Albuquerque. Brock was there."

"It's the same phone," McCrae said. "I just don't understand why the chief would have it in his desk. Unless he took it off someone during a search or an arrest."

"Or he has it because the cartel ordered him to recover it." Occam's razor and all that garbage. The simplest answer was usually the correct answer, and it wouldn't be the first time Cash had known law enforcement to get in bed with the very people they were publicly committed to taking down.

"No. No way. The chief isn't working for those bastards. Not in a million years." McCrae grabbed for the phone, then pulled back as Cash dodged the attempt. Frustrated was an understatement. The deputy was taking Cash's suggestion personally. "You don't know him like I do. That man bleeds blue through and through. He patrols on his off-hours. He helps anyone he can, even if it's just to rake Mrs. Baker's leaves out of her front yard. Hell, he's not even from here. He's a transplant from somewhere back east, but he's spent the past five years serving this town. Without him, it would've been overrun a long time ago."

"I have no doubt your chief does his job well, but we can't discount the possibility he's working for *Sangre por Sangre* on the side." Cash bagged the device. "Cartel informers are good at what they do. They're recruited because they can stay under the radar, get access civilians can't, and they're very good liars. It's hard to spot one unless you know what you're looking for."

"Let's say you're right. Okay? The chief—a man I've known and respected for half a decade and has a complete knowledge of the latest tech and forensics in investigative cases—is working for *Sangre por Sangre*." McCrae pointed to the phone. "Don't you think he'd be smart enough to get rid of this thing before someone caught on? Lock it up, at least?"

Elena rolled her bottom lip between her teeth and bit down, claiming Cash's attention in an instant. Given the choice between blackmailing a judge to get her brother back and going about this whole mess the long way, she'd shown her true colors. Courageous in the face of losing everything she'd fought for. Honorable. A hero in her own right. And damn, if that didn't make him love her more.

Love.

That single thought paralyzed him down to a cellular level. Hell, where had that come from? He wasn't in any position to feel anything for anyone but a Rottweiler. He'd loved someone once, and that kind of vulnerability had torn him to shreds with Wade's betrayal. He couldn't go through that again. Because emotions and feelings overrode any order, any assignment, any situation. If he couldn't do his job, people died. Cartels grew. And towns like Alpine Valley disappeared off the map.

But Elena had met him on the battlefield. She'd taken up position at his side and held her head high as the enemy had centered her and her family in the crosshairs. She'd gotten them out of the cartel's and her ex's stranglehold by risking her life for others. She'd backed his decision not to lower their tactics in line with the very people she hated most, and, yeah, he loved her for that. For all of that.

But everything between them had been built on a lie. And the part of him that missed having a partner that wasn't a K-9 who was scared of the dark— someone to joke with, to ease the weight of the world, to love—knew he and Elena would never work until he came clean about the night of the raid.

"The chief wouldn't have been able to get to the information on that phone without my passcode," she said. "Could be the only reason he hasn't handed it over. It wouldn't do him any good to give it up without knowing what was on it."

"She's right. Any good informant working for people like Metias knows leverage is their best bet of getting what they want out of the deal." Cash forced his head back in the game. They'd recovered the phone. They had to chance to cut off the head of the snake, but finding the device in the chief's desk exposed a variable they hadn't planned for. That the snake was actually a hydra. Cut off one head, two or more grow in its place. "If the chief couldn't access the intel Elena stored, he would've wanted to bide his time long enough to get the passcode before meeting with his handler."

"The chief helped me unload my things from the car that night I moved back." She raised that enigmatic gaze to Cash, and it was as though they were right back in his bed. With nothing but the two of them. "Metias must've tipped him off about what I'd done. I kept the phone on me instead of in my bags because I was terrified the cartel was coming for me. I hid it in the ruins the next day. The chief must've followed me to be able to make the switch."

"Or he could've been doing what the chief does and simply did you a favor by helping out." McCrae shoved his hand through a full head of hair. "This…

This is ridiculous. The chief doesn't have a handler, he isn't handing over information to the very people we're trying to protect this town from and he isn't some spy. The man barely says a word to the officers in this department. Our best bet is to hand the phone over to the DEA and their crime lab and let them deal with anything that comes of the information on it."

The deputy had a point. They'd involved Alpine Valley police by coming here instead of bringing the intel straight to the DEA. But the moment McCrae handed off the phone into evidence, they'd lose their leverage to bring Daniel home. "That could take weeks. Socorro is far more equipped to see this through."

"I can't just hand over a piece of evidence to a bunch of mercenaries in the hopes you'll keep us in the loop, Meyers." McCrae tried to hold back a laugh. The pressure was getting to him. He wasn't in any position to make these kinds of decisions. Could be one of the reasons the man hadn't seen a promotion in all the time he'd served Alpine Valley. "Do you have any idea what would happen to me? To my career?"

They were going in circles. Losing what precious little time Daniel Navarro had left. The boy had already been in the cartel's hands for three straight days. Long enough to make him forget the life he'd had before his abduction with the right psychological tactics.

"Then we eliminate the chief as a suspect right

now." Elena relieved Cash of the phone and flipped it open through the bag. The screen lit up, and she pressed a series of numbers through the plastic to gain access. Always one to take action rather than wait for a plan. It countered every instinct that'd been ingrained into him through his training, but following her lead had gotten them further than working out all the details ahead of time. "I took hundreds of photos of documents and names in the weeks I was married to Metias. If the chief's name or face isn't in any of them, we'll know who we can trust. It'll take some time, but it's better to know what we're getting into than to look over our shoulders for the rest of our lives."

She scanned through the photos, and with each passing second, the deputy seemed to get more agitated. They weren't breaking any laws. The phone belonged to Elena, but an official DEA investigation had been opened with the cartel's raid on the town. The chief could return any second, and McCrae would find himself in hot water for sharing intel outside of the department.

Cash couldn't explain it—the feeling they were missing something. Bear stared at him. She hadn't indicated anything suspicious, though she'd taken up sitting beside the deputy's desk corner. Like she was waiting for Cash's permission to proceed. She'd only done that one time before. Waited instead of charging full tilt at a threat. It'd been inside the warehouse where the DEA and Marine Corps had set up their staging area before her final assignment.

Her paws kneaded the carpet, just as they had in the hours before their entire world had changed. He didn't have reason to order her to search the trailer, but her behavior wasn't lining up. Though she hadn't worked in drug or explosive detection for over a year, Bear would never forget.

Something was off in this trailer.

Cash could feel it. He scanned along the filing cabinets lined up along one wall. If *Sangre por Sangre* had infiltrated the Alpine Valley police department, it stood to reason they'd want to keep an eye on developments from within. Surveillance, recording devices, wiretaps on the LAN lines. Socorro had utilized and worked with all of them. It'd be easy enough to spot.

"Here's something." Elena's face brightened with the potential of a lead. She glanced from McCrae to Cash, drawing them in with her excitement. "It's a list of handwritten names I found in Metias's desk. I originally thought it was a rundown of his aliases, but they're so different from each other. It makes more sense that they're other people he's keeping tabs on. Maybe informants?"

Cash couldn't get a good look at the list on an inch-and-a-half-by-one-inch pixelated screen, but she seemed to be able to make out the names well enough.

The deputy took a step toward his desk.

Bear's ears lifted away from her face slightly as she tracked McCrae's move from her position.

And it was then Cash knew.

Confusion cocked Elena's head back slightly. "The chief's name isn't on here. I've been through everything. No mention of him anywhere." Elena lowered the phone to her side. "But there is one name I recognize." She turned toward the deputy. "Yours."

A nervous laugh burst from McCrae's chest, and Cash reached for his weapon. Damn it. The deputy had made him surrender it at the door with a promise to give it back once they left the station. "That's insane, Elena. We've known each other since we were kids. You've eaten dinner with my family. You know I'd never work for people like the cartel. Come on. I'm the one who came to get you when you wanted to escape your marriage. This is all some sick game your ex is playing with you. You have to believe me."

Cash took a step forward, positioning himself closer to the deputy. "Elena, how did you reach McCrae when you needed out of Albuquerque?"

"I had to buy a phone Metias didn't know about. I messaged him." Elena's gaze widened. "With this phone."

"Well, I was really hoping to avoid this, but what are you going to do?" McCrae's innocence bled from his face as he withdrew his sidearm and took aim. At Elena. Bear's defenses instantly went on alert with a series of barks and warnings at the deputy. "You were right. An informant has to have some kind of leverage to get what he wants out of a deal with a cartel like *Sangre por Sangre*. So I'll be taking that phone now."

Chapter Twelve

"You son of a bitch. You knew. You knew what the cartel was going to do, and you let it happen anyway." How could she have been so blind? Cash had tried to warn her, but she hadn't wanted to see it. Until it was too late. "You knew they were going to take Daniel. He's only eight years old!"

She lunged to get her hands on the friend she believed she'd known as well as herself, but Cash held her back. Brock loaded a round into his weapon, and her heart shot into her throat. Would he really shoot her? After all the years she'd trusted him?

"Now, Elena. Don't be trying to blame all this pain and suffering on me," the deputy said. "If you'd just been a good girl like you were supposed to and kept your nose out of cartel business, Metias wouldn't have had any reason to send his men to look for you and this phone. Lucky for me, I'm observant. I didn't recognize the number you messaged me from that night in Albuquerque. Took some doing, but I was able to match it to a cash purchase on a day you were seen in town. But it was the way you held on to it as though it were a lifeline after I picked you up outside of the city. I put two and two together. You were hiding something."

Elena squeezed the phone in her hand harder. The plastic protested under her grip, and she wanted nothing more in that moment than to destroy it so the weasel had nothing to offer *Sangre por Sangre*. Only then she'd have nothing to use as her own leverage to get Daniel back. Was this how Cash had felt when he'd learned what his brother had done? So much anger that had nowhere to go? Building until she feared she'd explode from the pressure?

"So you started informing on Elena to her ex." Cash angled himself in front of her, but it wouldn't be enough. Bullets were known to go through bodies even as massive as his, and she wasn't sure he could take any more after what the cartel had already done to him.

"Well, subterfuge certainly doesn't come quite as easily to me as it does to you, Elena. I kept an eye on you, trying to figure out what it was you were up to. Call it an inner sense of curiosity. Days went by, then a week. I gave you as many chances as I could, but when you still didn't tell me what was going on, I followed you up to those ruins." Brock cut his attention from Elena to Cash. Trying to mentally work out who he'd shoot first. Her chest tightened at the thought of any of those choices. But sooner or later, he would make a choice. "Found your phone hidden in the wall. You were smart to password protect it, but that left me in a predicament. Because I didn't have anything I could give Metias in exchange for what I wanted most. You could've trusted me, Elena. We could've been a team. You, me, we could've started the life together we'd always talked about. I just needed you to trust me. Now we're going to have to do this the hard way."

"Talked about?" Her stomach turned at the thought. She'd known. For years. The signs had been there since before she'd gotten married and let herself be swept away. Brock had asked her on dates in high school, but she'd wanted out of Alpine Valley, and he'd set his heart on becoming a police officer. They'd been friends. Movie nights, high school dances, hikes together. He'd listened to all the unimportant things she thought she wanted out of her life, like moving away, traveling the world, making something more of herself than a small-town New Mexico girl. There'd been countless nights the two of them had just stared at the stars from the hood of his dad's car wondering what the universe held for them. She'd celebrated his acceptance into the police force. Once Metias had entered the picture, he'd asked her to not go through with her engagement. But the only other option had been staying in a town she was desperate to leave, with a man she'd never see as anything more than a friend.

Only now that friend wanted something more.

"I do trust you." Elena took a step toward Brock, toward the gun barrel slightly shaking in his hand. She hadn't been able to convince Cash of her interest the time she'd lifted the keys for his SUV from his pocket, but he was a trained military contractor. Brock… Brock was a nobody from Alpine Valley who hadn't even graduated at the middle of his class from the police academy.

"Elena." Cash's warning sliced through her. There was so much power in that single whisper of her name. She'd read once a name was the sweetest word someone could ever speak to a person, and they were right. Her name falling from his mouth drilled through the pain and anguish and balled into a tight knot of hope. With that one warning, he was promising to fight for her, to protect her, to have her back and follow through with recovering Daniel from the cartel. But it was so much more than that. It was a map of their future together. One where the things they'd been through didn't hurt anymore. Where she didn't have to bear the weight of pain and injustice alone. It promised healing and Oreos that weren't laced with Bear's allergy medication. He was promising a partnership born of love, and she wanted that. With him.

"It's okay. He's not going to hurt me. Because I know what he's planning to negotiate with the cartel for." Elena raised her hands in surrender, pinching the phone between her thumb and palm. "Me."

"That's one of the reasons I've always liked you,

Elena. You accept people for who they really are."
Brock motioned toward her with the gun. "Now,
here's what's going to happen. You're going to hand
me that phone, then you and me are walking out of
here. We'll use what you gathered to take down *Sangre por Sangre* and get your brother back. Together.
Like it should've been from the beginning. I tried to
warn you about Metias, but you wouldn't listen. But
you're listening now, aren't you?"

"Over my dead body." Cash moved to intercept,
but Brock seemed to breathe new life into his gun
hold. The weapon raised a fraction of an inch and
centered on Cash. Bear exposed her teeth, a terrifying
growl vibrating through her hundred-pound frame.
She didn't like when people threatened her handler.

"That's far enough." Brock redirected his aim, and
it took everything inside of Elena not to step between
Bear and the gun. "One more step and the doggy
gets hurt. You wouldn't want that, would you, Meyers? From what I could find on you, the two of you
have been through quite enough already since your
brother died. I wouldn't want to break up the band."

"Brock, you don't have to do this. Okay? Nobody
has to get hurt." Elena took another step to claim the
deputy's attention. Because it was the only way to
ensure Cash and Bear got out of here. "You have me.
Let them go, and the phone is yours." Acid churned
in her gut. "I'll be yours. Just like you wanted. All
you have to do is let them leave."

"Elena, no." Cash's voice dipped into dangerous territory. "You're not going anywhere."

"You think I'm that foolish? I know you'd say anything to make sure you were the only one who suffered. Because that's who you are. That's what makes you so easy to manipulate, Elena." Brock's mouth thinned into a smile she'd never seen before. A combination of amusement and corruption that set her defenses on high alert.

"But would you still feel the same way if you learned Cash Meyers was the one who failed to warn Alpine Valley the cartel was making their move the night of the raid?" His low laugh infused Elena's nerves with dread. "Did you ever ask him what he did in the Marine Corps? What his job for that security company is? He's a forward observer, Elena. He's the one who tracks the cartel's movements to give towns like ours a chance of evacuating. Makes me wonder what he was doing the night *Sangre por Sangre* took Daniel from you. Where was his warning?"

What? No. That didn't… That didn't make sense. Cash would've told her. Elena turned to put him in her sights, waiting for him to explain. To give her the answer she found herself so desperately needing in that moment. "Cash?"

His guard was back in place. The one that'd taken her days to work through. He held her gaze long enough to convince her of the truth. Brock wasn't lying. Not this time.

That cutting sense of betrayal she'd felt realizing her lifelong friend had given her up to the cartel was nothing compared to the twist of an invisible blade through her heart, handled by the man in front of her. The one she'd let hold her through the night, who'd saved her life and put a fantasy of real partnership and a future in her head. The one who'd convinced her she didn't have to be this broken remnant of a marriage she never should've gotten into in the first place. Heat assaulted her then. Shame, hot and undeniable, worked beneath her skin and eviscerated everything she thought she'd known about him. Her ex had made her feel small and worthless. Weak. Cash had given her the chance and the guts to be strong.

But it'd all been a lie from the beginning.

Her heart crumpled right there in her chest. Beaten black and blue to the point she wasn't sure it could ever be revitalized. "It's true, isn't it?"

Cash finally broke his vow of silence. "Elena, I'm—"

"I'm sorry. We are simply out of time for heartfelt apologies." Brock struck without warning. He fisted Elena's hair and dragged her back into his chest. She reached up to pry his hands free, but the harder she fought, the more force he used.

Violence spread through Cash's eyes, and she swore every muscle in his body flexed under the pressure. "You're going to want to get your hands off her. Now."

Bear lunged without a command. She clamped onto Brock's arm. His scream triggered a high-pitched ringing in her ears a split second before the gun went off.

The bullet threw Cash back.

He hit the floor.

Blood bloomed across his T-shirt in an instant.

"No!" Elena tried to reach him, but the deputy only held on tighter. "Cash!"

"Get off of me!" Brock's foot connected with Bear's ribs, and Elena's would-be protector belted an injured whine as the Rottweiler rolled across the floor. Unmoving.

Elena threw back her elbow as she'd seen Cash do in the middle of a fight, connecting with bone and cartilage, but the deputy recovered faster than she expected. She hadn't hit him hard enough to break his nose.

Brock sucked in air between his teeth as he surveyed the bloody damage done to his forearm. "That's enough of that. Looks like our ride is here." He shoved her toward the trailer's front door, a glimpse of a large SUV taking shape through the glass. "And, believe me, we don't want to keep him waiting."

OH, HELL. DYING HURT.

He hadn't liked it the first time an assignment had blown up in his face, and he certainly didn't enjoy it now. Cash managed to roll off his bullet-ridden shoulder. Blood soaked into the already-stained industrial carpet underneath him. The shot had gone straight through. Sitting up, he clamped a hand over the wound. Son of a bitch.

Deputy McCrae had been the informant.

Not the chief as they'd been led to believe.

The pieces of the puzzle were starting to make sense. He'd just put them together too late. But there was still time. For Elena. For her brother. A dark outline of hair and muscle whined from across the trailer, and dread took over. "Bear."

Cash crawled on one hand and both knees toward her. She flinched at his approach. "Shhh. It's me. It's okay."

The lean muscles behind her legs and down her back relaxed, but only slightly. He ran his good hand along the length of her side. He'd blacked out from the impact of the bullet. "What happened, huh? What'd he do to you?"

Bear set her head back against the floor, blinking those big dark eyes he trusted with his life. She'd tried to protect Elena. That much was clear. Following an order he'd given days ago. A line of blood stained the hair around her mouth. She'd taken a bite out of McCrae. The bastard had been lucky she hadn't torn him to pieces. Another whine broke through the pound of his heartbeat behind his ears.

"I'm sorry." He wasn't sure who he'd meant the apology for. For Bear, in pain and unable to move from possible broken ribs to match his own, or Elena.

The hurt in her expression had seared itself into his brain. It'd been the last thing he'd seen before the bullet had ripped through him and was the only image in his head now. He'd done nothing but ask her to trust him these past few days, and he'd broken that trust. He'd betrayed her as easily as his brother had corrupted their joint DEA mission.

Corrupted.

That was what he was. The fear there was something waiting inside of him, something dark and evil and defective, had kept him on the edge to prove he wasn't anything like his brother. To take on more assignments, to push himself harder than the rest of the team. Thousands in donations, hundreds of hours of community service, countless volunteer opportunities whenever he got the chance—it'd all been for nothing. None of it had erased that hollowness that'd taken over Wade's conscience. And now, he was just like his little brother.

A fraud.

The night of the raid. It was still so clear in his mind. He'd had no other leads in recovering Wade's body for over a year. Over and over again until the days blended together and hope had disintegrated, he and Bear had hit the dirt the moment the sun crested the plateaus. They'd searched through blistering heat, sunless mornings and dozens of grids laid out over the course of hundreds of square miles. Then Socorro's source within the cartel had passed along coordinates and sworn his intel was good. And it had been.

The remains had been picked over to the point the buzzards hadn't even bothered circling anymore. Unrecognizable. While the elements took their pound of flesh, the body's clothing had protected some of the dehydrated skin beneath a pair of cargo pants and the man's shoes. Teeth had been removed. The sun had dried up any blood left in the body. Not even Doc Piel would've been able to do anything to rehydrate the body's fingertips to get prints. But Cash had known the moment he'd seen the tattoo. The broken outline of a doughnut reading *A-dough-rable*.

There was supposed to be a sense of relief, of closure, from finally completing his personal mission, but it'd never come. He'd wanted something more as he'd stared at his brother's remains. But bodies couldn't talk. They couldn't apologize or explain or argue. He'd waited. He'd waited for Wade to stand up, to brush himself off and crack that ridiculous grin of his, but all Cash had gotten was a dead man. Until hatred and grief and pain had exploded to the point he found himself screaming into the night. Bear had simply lain down next to Wade as he raged. It wasn't until an hour later—maybe more—that he'd caught sight of the fires. By then it'd been too late.

The cartel had taken his brother's identity as a final nail in his coffin, but Wade's corrupted legacy would live on regardless. His actions would continue to ripple out. Affecting the families of the men and women who'd died in that explosion, strengthening the cartel's reputation, helping organizations like *Sangre por Sangre* spread like the disease they were by weakening law enforcement one mission at a time. All stemming from one choice. One man. The person Cash had trusted most in the world.

And now his choice to keep the truth from Elena about that night would follow the same track. It'd separated her family and lost them a vital piece of their lives. It'd paved the way for Metias and *Sangre por Sangre* to find Elena. And it'd undermined Socorro's ability to protect the people and the towns systematically becoming targets of the cartel.

Recovering Wade's body was supposed to fix everything. But it hadn't. It'd only made things worse and distracted him from what should've been his only priority: Elena.

But he wouldn't let her pay for his mistakes.

She deserved better. Better than Metias. Better than McCrae. And better than him.

Cash set his thumb beneath one of Bear's ears— her favorite spot to be scratched—then followed the ridge of her collar to the emergency SOS signal embedded in the leather. He collapsed beside her. "I'm going to get you out of here. Okay? Just as soon as I remember what it feels like to use this arm."

She directed that dark gaze to his, then let her eyes slip closed as he threaded one hand beneath her

neck and the other under her hip. Tucking his knees
beneath him, Cash braced for the pain that came
with hauling her into his chest. Blood seeped from
his wound, faster than before. The quicker his pulse
picked up, the harder his heart pumped out blood
through the injury, but he wouldn't stop.

Because this wasn't finished.

McCrae might've gotten what he wanted with the
intel Elena had stolen, but it wouldn't be enough for
the cartel. Nothing could ever be enough, and they
would never stop. Not until there wasn't anything
left to control.

Cash stumbled forward, his injured leg barely
taking his and Bear's weights combined. One knee
gave out, and he dropped at the corner of McCrae's
desk. His elbow slammed onto the cheap faux wood.
Nerves screamed in protest at the pressure, but it was
there Cash noted a sprinkle of white powder dusting
the edge of the desk.

Bear had sat in this exact spot. She hadn't been
waiting for an order. She'd tried signaling Cash to the
presence of drugs, and he'd missed it. It made sense
now. He'd run a background check on the deputy
for the same signs he'd noted in Wade's financials
and phone records, but paperwork didn't always re-
flect drug use.

Cartels these days were careful. They didn't
need corners. The drug game had turned into a
boutique-style delivery service, usually under the

cover of some other business. Pizza, flowers, internet orders—sometimes more than one. Text a number, place an order, pay with a credit card or checking account. McCrae would've been subject to background checks throughout his career. He'd known exactly how to hide his dirty little habit. From his friends, family, his chief. And now he had Elena.

Movement registered at the station's front door.

"Lucy, I'm home." Jocelyn Carville cleared the room in a fraction of a second and crossed the distance between them. Her hand instantly went to the butt of her weapon. Maverick raced through the room, circling Cash with an added bounce to his step. "Damn it. I swear one of these days I'm going to roll up to find you dead. Tell me what happened."

"The deputy happened." Cash managed to get to his feet with her taking some of Bear's weight. "Son of a bitch has been informing on Elena since she came back to Alpine Valley. He took her and gave me a bullet as an early birthday present. My guess is he's headed straight back to the cartel. Background check was clear, but check this out." He nodded at the thin powder coating the desk.

She whistled low, gaining Maverick's attention. The German shepherd sniffed along the desk then sneezed with a violent shake of his head before pawing at the carpet. "Well, it's not drywall dust. You think he's a frequent consumer?"

"Enough to cloud his judgment when it comes to

getting in bed with *Sangre por Sangre*." He should've seen it. McCrae's determination to blackmail a judge for a geofence warrant, his offer to take the phone into evidence. Both had been to buy himself as much time as possible. He'd been the one to switch out the device for a replica and plant it in the chief's desk. "Joce, I need you to take Bear."

Understanding hit as they carried the Rottweiler to Jocelyn's waiting SUV. He could see it in the way the logistics officer lowered her gaze to the bullet hole in his shoulder, then came straight back to his face. "You can't be serious. You're injured. Running after her in this condition isn't going to work out for either of you."

"I can't leave her to fight them alone. You know that." Cash groaned low and deep, mirroring Bear's moan, as they got her into the cargo area of Jocelyn's vehicle. Maverick hopped in and lay down beside his K-9 teammate. Protective and concerned. Cash added pressure to his wound in hopes of controlling the bleeding. In vain.

"You're out of your mind if you think I'm going to let you fight them alone in this condition," she said. "Elena's at least in one piece."

"I've got a field kit in the car." Pain stabbed down his arm. He wasn't sure how much a field kit would help, but it was better than bleeding out in the middle of a cul-de-sac. "You can stay to help patch me up, but I'm not asking. I'm telling. I'm going after Elena. So

I need you to get Bear back to the vet. I can't do this if I'm worried about her. Understand?"

Jocelyn cut her attention to Maverick and back. She'd make the same choice if it came right down to it. They all would. She grabbed her field kit from behind Bear and rolled it out. "Fine. But if you die, I'm going to tell everyone you watch rom-coms when you think no one is awake."

"You're not supposed to know about that," he said. "I was careful."

"Oh, but I do." She twisted off the lid to the bottle of alcohol and dumped a good amount onto a piece of gauze, waiting for him to make the next move. "And I have proof. So you better come back alive."

Chapter Thirteen

Someone would find Cash before it was too late.

He wasn't dead. He wasn't, but no matter how many times she'd begged the men in the SUV to go back, she'd been ignored.

Deputy McCrae's knee rubbed against hers from his position beside her. Not Brock. The man sitting next to her wasn't her friend. He wasn't her confidant or the one she'd relied on to get her out of Albuquerque and her marriage. She didn't know him anymore. He'd taken her trust and twisted it into something ugly and left Cash with a bullet in the process.

Her lip throbbed in rhythm with her racing heart rate. She'd tried to claw her way out the back of the SUV, to escape as distance shrank down the police station through the back window, but McCrae had been prepared for her to fight. And not opposed to hurting her to get what he wanted. Bastard.

"Cheer up, Elena. The dog is still alive." McCrae knocked his knee into hers as though they were simply joking about that cheesy horror movie they'd watched together last Halloween. "I'm not a total monster."

She had a few recent experiences to refute him, but there was no point. Squeezing herself against the window, she tried to drown the nausea churning in her gut. Every touch, every look, every word out of his mouth made her sick. Alpine Valley faded as the trees thinned along the borders of town. Coming home had been her only option after she'd left Albuquerque. She hadn't appreciated it. Not really. The protective cliffs, the shade the trees had provided all her life, the sheer beauty of an oasis dead center in one of the hottest deserts in existence. "It's not the dog I'm worried about."

Though Bear had taken a solid kick to the ribs. The Rottweiler hadn't moved an inch as McCrae dragged Elena out of the trailer. The idea of Cash losing his partner hurt despite the fact he'd been partly responsible for the pain and anguish she and her family had been through. What had McCrae called him? A forward observer. The man in charge of seeing the threat coming from a mile away, of ensuring towns like Alpine Valley had warning before the strike. Like an air raid siren for tornadoes. Though something had kept Cash from warning them the night of the raid. Maybe if he had, she might've been able to get Daniel to safety. Maybe they could've escaped the violence and the loss and betrayal.

Tears pricked at her eyes.

"Oh, come now. You can't honestly tell me you're worried about that Socorro thug. I did you a favor," McCrae said. "If you think about it, he's the reason the cartel got their hands on Daniel in the first place. You should be thanking me. Mercenaries like him are nothing but *Sangre por Sangre* soldiers on an imaginary leash. You don't want that in your life."

"And what about corrupt cops?" she asked. "How are they any different?"

His laugh was all the warning she had before McCrae gripped the back of her neck and thrust her face into the back of the front passenger seat. Lightning struck behind her eyes from the momentum, but her nose was largely saved by the leather. It took a few seconds for her vision to clear, but Elena caught the driver's gaze on her from the rearview mirror. She'd met him before. Not in the compound. In Albuquerque. One of the men her husband had brought around the house before she'd run. She couldn't read his expression, but she knew one thing for certain: he wouldn't help her.

"Don't worry, Elena." McCrae unpocketed the phone he'd taken from her. "I'm going to take good care of you. You'll see."

Gravity took hold of her insides as the SUV angled down into the compound construction site. Dirt kicked along and pinged off of the SUV's doors though the engineers and excavators had halted work on the actual structure. Dread forced acid into her throat. Cash had risked his life to get her out of this building. Now she might never see the outside of it again.

Her heart threatened to pound straight out of her chest at the thought. Of not seeing him again. He'd lied to her about the night of the raid. From the very beginning, he'd witnessed what had happened to homes and families displaced because he'd failed to do his job. But though she wanted to hate him as much as she hated her ex or Deputy McCrae, he wasn't like them. No matter what McCrae said. Cash wasn't just some soldier with an imaginary leash. He was a protector. One of the very best.

Without him and Bear, she wouldn't have made it out of Alpine Valley that first night. Or survived Metias's psychological torture. Without Cash, she'd have never found a reason to laugh or let someone just hold her through the night. And while nothing physical had happened between them apart from that kiss, those hours in his arms had fortified her in a way she never thought possible. Had given her hope and a reason to keep fighting. Not for others. For herself.

Sunlight vanished as the driver pulled into the underground parking garage, and every cell in her body went on high alert. She couldn't see him through the dark tint of the windows, but he was there. Waiting for her. Metias. She could feel it. She rocked forward as the SUV was thrown into Park, and the air in her chest evaporated.

"Time to claim what's mine." McCrae reached across her lap and shoved the door open. On the other side, her husband stood to greet them.

Only there was no smile this time. No warm welcome or the familiar mask of deception he liked to hide behind. Metias stood proud with his arms at his sides, his expression as severe as the time he'd caught her going through the mail. And a pistol gripped in one hand. "You and I have much to discuss, *mi amor*." He cocked his head to one side, looking past her. "I take it you've brought me what I asked for, Deputy."

"Got it right here." McCrae nudged her out the door, and Elena was forced to face the man she'd run from not once but twice. The deputy kept a tight lock on her arm, but she wasn't going to run this time. "Took some doing, but she says it's everything she collected."

"Bueno." Metias nodded and two soldiers materialized from the shadows. "Then you and I have concluded our business. Elena."

Her ex said her name like calling a dog to heel. It was nothing compared to the way Cash made her feel. Safe. Strong. Confident. Metias didn't care about her. She was a trophy in his eyes. Something to be won through the pain of others. And Cash... He'd put her first in every scenario they'd gone into together. Ensured she had a place to sleep, food to eat. Only asked to touch her with her permission instead of taking what he felt he was owed. Yeah, there'd been a moment—maybe a few—she'd questioned his motives, but the difference between the two men with actual power over her was clear.

One used domination. The other let her choose her path, and she loved him for it. She loved Cash, and there wasn't a damn thing McCrae or Metias could do about it. They'd taken everything from her, but they couldn't take that, and the second she figured out how to get the hell out of here, she'd find him.

"Now hold on there, honcho. I don't believe we have." McCrae moved the phone back into his uniform pocket. He tucked her into his side body. "I went through an awful lot to get this information for you. Had to shoot a man. That requires a lot of cleanup on my end. Our business isn't even close to concluded."

"You want to change the deal." Thin skin around Metias's eyes seemed more translucent as though a demon were about to stretch through and possess him from within. "I'll tell you what, Officer…"

"Deputy. McCrae." The deputy enunciated every syllable. His grip tightened around her arm, punishing and painful.

Elena didn't dare move. Didn't dare to take her next breath. She knew what it meant to disobey the man in front of them, and every instinct she owned screamed at her to get as far from the deputy as possible. She tried to wrench her arm free, but there was nowhere she could run.

"McCrae." Metias let the deputy's name roll off his tongue with constrained flair. "I admire your passion. You believe you deserve something for your hard work. I commend that. I've promoted men within my organization for showing such vigor." Her ex closed the distance between them slowly, gauging his prey. He motioned to her lip. "I take it you are the one who did this to Elena. She's stubborn, no?"

McCrae's chest puffed up as big as a bird's in mating season. A smile she'd always been disarmed by pinched the edges of his mouth. "Had to throw her into the back of the headrest to stop that mouth of hers."

Metias's laugh belted from his lungs, hard and brash. But when the laugh died, so did the humor on his face. Her ex raised his weapon and fired. Once. Twice.

The deputy's body jerked beside her, and soon his grip disappeared from her arm entirely. Blood splattered onto her shirt, neck and face just before he collapsed to the ground. McCrae stared up at her as his final breath leaked from the holes in his chest. Dead.

"I believe that concludes our business." Metias used the barrel of his weapon to signal one of the men waiting in the wings. *"Consigue el teléfono."* Get the phone. The soldier did as he was asked, pulling her phone from McCrae's jacket, and in a fraction of a second, her life—and that of her brother's—was entirely in her ex-husband's hands. One of which he was extending out to her right then. "Welcome to our new home, *mi esposa*."

"I'm not your wife, Metias," she said. "I don't care what the courts say."

"Let's hear what you have to say after you see the gift I brought for you." He snapped his fingers as men in power did, expecting for his needs to be instantly met. And they were. A second pair of men stepped free of the shadows cast by the underground garage's overhang.

With her brother between them.

Metias rounded behind her, his mouth too close to her ear. "I can forgive the fact you stole from me, Elena, but I will not tolerate you making a fool of me. This has gone on long enough. I gave you a choice the last time we were together. I'm still waiting for your answer. Come home to me, make this right and your brother goes free. Refuse—" her ex raised his weapon again, to the side of her head "—and you both die."

HIS LEG ZINGED with numbness as the compound came into view.

Cash kept low along the crater's rim, looking down into the construction site. The trek across the desert upped the chances of finishing him off, but signaling the cartel of his approach would only sign his death warrant sooner.

He dragged his backpack higher up his shoulder.

Elena was down there. He felt it as if she were

calling to him. The connection they'd built in a matter of days pulled him unlike anything he'd ever experienced. It wasn't physical or mental or emotional. It was all of those things combined into something otherworldly and terrifying. He'd loved and lost. But this… This was worth risking his life for. Worth risking everything for.

They'd survived despite having no layout of that compound, not knowing how many soldiers they were up against or what they were getting themselves into. Because they'd worked as a team. He'd always been the kind of operator who needed a plan, who'd worked out every detail so he could predict the oncoming threat. But if there was one thing he'd learned since taking this assignment, it was that nothing was impossible. Not as long as he and Elena were together.

Cash surveyed the site for movement, but if the cartel had regrouped at the half-finished compound, satellites picked anything up. No movement. No signs of life or an ambush. But experience warned him not to take enemy lines at face value.

He dug his heels into the dirt and descended the steep incline. Rock and dust infiltrated his gear and slowed him down at the bottom. Taking cover behind one of the excavators, Cash swung his backpack forward and pried the zipper open. *Sangre por Sangre* would've narrowed down his and Elena's entry point from their last visit to the compound. There were no guarantees the override code would work for the security system any longer. He needed another plan to get in.

One that brought the cartel out.

He handled the explosive and detonator carefully as he attached it beneath the excavator's operator's seat. Then moved on to the next and the next. His senses rocketed into overdrive as he tried to keep out of sight. His injured shoulder tingled from overuse. Jocelyn had done a fine job cleaning him up, but chances of infection and blood loss were still high. He had to keep moving.

For Elena. For her brother.

The guilt that'd eaten at him since the moment he'd hauled her into the back of his SUV the night of the raid reared its ugly head and wouldn't let go.

Wade hadn't deserved his obsession all these past months, and if Cash hadn't been out in the middle of the desert looking for his body, Elena and Daniel might not be in danger now. His brother had betrayed everything they'd stood for growing up and had forgotten their agreement to fight for justice and change the world for the better. What had gone wrong? When was the moment Wade made his choice to denounce everything they'd sacrificed for?

A low growl escaped his chest as he got eyes on the compound's underground parking garage. It didn't matter. His brother was dead. Cash wasn't ever getting an answer, but he couldn't help but imagine the countless scenarios in which Wade would've crossed that line. The same line Cash would cross to save the woman he loved if she required it of him.

Understanding hit there—in the shadow of the cartel's physical manifestation of resources and control. His brother was younger, but he'd always taken on the role of protecting Cash when they'd been kids. Like the time Cash had climbed into the skeleton of an abandoned barn to outrun a group of boys determined to beat him to a pulp. Hadn't done much good. They'd thrown rocks to try to bring him down. One had sliced through his eyebrow and left behind the scar he had today. Wade charged into that building and punched the leader square in the face. Knocked the kid out cold. The others hadn't even dared try to take Wade on after that.

A heaviness ached behind Cash's sternum. He hadn't thought about that day in a long time. Too angry. Too busy. Too…empty. His brother had fought by his side the day of that task force mission. Always had. And that was what hurt the most. Wade hadn't just betrayed his oath to serve and protect his country and the people at the mercy of the cartel. He'd betrayed Cash. Walked him straight into that ambush, knowing what waited for him on the other side.

The memories were still there, right on the cusp. He'd played them over and over in his head, and that same gut feeling of a setup took up residence as he approached the garage. He shook it off. Only difference between then and now? He knew what he was getting himself into this time. And what he would do to get Elena and her little brother out.

Blood seeped through the gauze and T-shirt protecting the wound in his shoulder, but the pain had receded in the past few minutes. He'd take full advantage.

Cement overhung the entrance with a barely-there security system blocking vehicles without a keycard from driving down into the belly of the beast. Still no sign of *Sangre por Sangre* soldiers. He made quick work of the remaining explosive charges in his bag, setting them around the perimeter. From the layout he'd catalogued during their first visit to the site, he mapped Metias's office on the far side of the complex. Cash surveyed the spacing between devices, then jogged clear of the building. The cartel had somehow blocked his emergency SOS signal two days ago. He wasn't going to make the assumption one would get through now. Unpocketing the radio he'd pried from the console of his SUV, he switched it to the channel he needed. "When in doubt, have a backup plan."

He hit the push-to-talk button.

The charges detonated simultaneously. Cement, dirt and glass ripped through the air like a series of volcanoes ridding themselves of debris. A wave of pressure from the blast raced across the desert floor and shoved Cash back. But he didn't have time to watch his work unravel. The entire garage had been swallowed by failing framing and cement. Boulder-sized chunks crumbled away from the main supports and exploded on impact. He dodged the first one. Then barely missed the second as he sprinted into the collapse. A wall of heat slammed into him as darkness overtook his vision.

The building's security system screeched high alert and triggered the sprinklers overhead. He navigated through the blast site and into a corridor still standing, then unholstered his weapon. Voices echoed down the hall to his position. No bodies in the debris. The blast had done its job in knocking out the cartel's main escape, but that still left him to deal with the panicked soldiers responding to the alarm.

Water pooled beneath his boots and streaked down his face as he moved. Twisting from one side to the other, he cleared each door branching off the main hallway. A loop of one memory—of him and Wade clearing a building a hundred miles from here—overlapped the onslaught of blaring noise and thundering response.

Two soldiers turned the corner up ahead, and Cash's finger automatically tightened on the trigger. They both took aim, but he was faster. Each bullet found its mark. The metallic *tink* of casings hitting the floor shoved him back into the present. The here and now. Where the only thing that mattered was getting to Elena.

His shoulder ached every second he fought gravity to keep his arms up and his hold tight around the gun. Sprinkler water infiltrated his vision as he cleared the next corner and moved on a trajectory to the back of the building. Bear would've done her share to make sure the path was clear, but he'd have to rely on his own instincts now.

The wall six inches from his face exploded in a rain of bullets.

The impact kicked up dust.

Cash pulled back to keep himself from taking another bullet. A series of clicks registered through the rhythmic silence of the alarm. He rushed the soldier whose gun had jammed ten feet away and cocked his elbow back to clock him dead between the eyes. The recruit crumpled as quickly as the structure's garage had, and Cash confiscated his weapon. "Stay down."

A seismic rumble seemed to ripple through the walls. Cash set his hand against the nearest column to keep his balance. He'd taken out the main supports under the garage. It was only a matter of time before the front half of the building collapsed in on itself. He just hoped he had enough time.

He set one foot in front of the other. The strap of the automatic rifle dug into his shoulder with every step. But it wouldn't slow him down. Another shift of the building had him picking up the pace. He was working blind, only able to rely on the fractured memories of his first visit to the compound with a concussion, but they would have to be enough.

He wasn't leaving without Elena or her brother.

He wouldn't fail her as he'd failed Wade.

He wouldn't allow their bodies to be left in the middle of the desert for him to find months from now.

Because the truth was, he should've been there for Wade. He'd known it since the moment he had recovered his brother's body in the middle of the New Mexican desert. He should've been more involved in his brother's life. Listened better. Taken the time to check in more often rather than losing himself in the next assignment. Maybe then Wade would've trusted him with whatever he'd gotten himself into. They could've put their heads together to get him out.

And Elena… Hell. He didn't know what would happen between them when this was over and danger wasn't waiting to ambush them at every turn. But he was willing to find out. Willing to put the obsession aside, cut back on the number of assignments he took on for Socorro, face the hurt and the pain for a chance to start anew. To do whatever it took to keep her in his life.

Her confidence in him, in the kind of man he was, was the only thing keeping his head above water. She'd dropped into his life at the precise moment he'd needed her the most, given him a chance to prove he could overcome that corruption he and Wade shared deep down. It wasn't the donations and service that defined his goodness. It was her. She'd exposed a piece of him he'd wanted to bury forever, and he'd do whatever it took to earn her trust back. To earn her love. She'd brought him out into the light, and Cash suddenly found himself afraid of the dark.

He checked the rounds left in the gun's magazine and carved through the building without stopping. "I'm coming, Elle. Just hold on a little while longer."

Chapter Fourteen

The building shook beneath her.

Elena clutched onto her brother just as she had the night of the raid, clamping a hand over his mouth to quiet his sobs. He'd assumed more scrapes and bruises since that last time she'd seen him, but he was alive. He was here. In her arms. They were going to make it out of this. "It's going to be okay. I've got you."

Words were all she had. Because unless she was sure one of these walls made up the exterior structure and magically created a hole in it, they weren't going anywhere. Still, her heart believed them. She threaded her fingers into his hair.

The alarms drowned out the sound of Metias's order, but the three men on guard around the room seemed to be able to discern his instructions. They each peeled away from their fearless leader and headed for the door, guns clutched against their chests.

Sprinklers hissed from overhead and drenched them within seconds. Something had happened. Maybe an explosion or a fire. An accident? Had Socorro gotten news of what'd happened to Cash and decided to carry out a raid of their own? Her mind raced with the possibilities. None of it mattered. It was the opportunity she'd been waiting for. A distraction the cartel wouldn't be able to ignore.

Metias wiped the thin veil of water from his face, baring his teeth like a wild animal warning an oncoming predator. "The two of you are coming with me. Let's go."

"No." She wasn't sure if her voice carried over the blare of the security system screaming for them to evacuate.

Pulling an oversize gleaming silver pistol from beneath his white suit jacket, Metias lunged for Daniel when neither of them moved at his insistence. He went to tear her brother out of her arms, but Elena stepped between them.

"Get away from him!" She moved Daniel behind her. She'd let him go to men like Metias once. She wouldn't let it happen again. Water soaked through her clothing and down into bone. It froze her from the outside in, but there was a raging heat already simmering beneath her skin. One she'd left dormant for far too long. "You don't get to touch him. Or me. Ever. Do you understand? We will never be what you want us to be. I'm not coming back, Metias. I'm not your wife anymore. I don't love you, and if you think I'll subject myself to you because you threaten me into submission, I'll fight. Every second of every day, I will try to get away from you. I don't care if you lock me in another cellar or the trunk of a car or whatever else the hell you have planned for me."

The fire overtook her then, countering the cold. Bolstering her strength and chasing back the doubt clawing for attention.

She clamped her jaw to control the tremors rolling through her. "I give you my word—I will make your life a living hell. You think you have enemies now? You have no idea what I will do to you if you lay another hand on Daniel or me."

Shock smoothed Metias's expression into something unreadable and foreign. It was only with a slight crack of his smile that she realized she'd gotten through to him.

She should've known by now that smile warned of pain.

He brought his pistol up. The metal slammed into the side of her face and knocked her off balance. Throbbing agony ripped across her temple and scalp as she fell.

"Lena!" Daniel tried to catch her in his tiny arms as she hit the floor. He dug his fingers into her arm, trying to tug her over his lap, but he wasn't strong enough.

Her vision went black for a series of breaths. The loss exaggerated Metias's footsteps as he crouched beside her. Water squished—too loud—in her ears. Warm liquid slithered into her hairline. Blood.

"If you think three days in a cellar without food and water is the worst I can do to you, *mi amor*, you are sadly mistaken." He pinched the edges of her mouth in a strong grip, pulling her upper body off the floor as her eyesight cleared. "I told you before. Nobody walks away from me. As for Daniel, well… There's no reason for you to fight me if you have nothing to live for." Metias raised the gun and took aim. At her brother.

"No!" Elena latched onto her ex's gun arm and shoved him back as hard as she could. The gun exploded mere inches from its target. Daniel's scream drilled through her a split second before Metias slammed his forehead against hers. A wave of pain and dizziness rattled her from the neck down, but she only tightened her hold on the bastard's arm. "Daniel, run!"

Everything blurred as Metias slammed her into the nearest wall. Her head snapped back and made contact with the cement. The gun fell from his grip and hit the floor with a thud, out of reach. A strong hand wrapped around her neck and squeezed. He had her pinned there, her vision growing dark against the red emergency lighting. The alarm warbled in her ears. She couldn't breathe, couldn't think. Pressure from the air locked in her chest built just below his hand, and she scratched at his face with everything she had to get free.

"Get away from my sister!" Movement from behind Metias's shoulder claimed her attention right before Daniel swung something heavy into the back of the man's head.

The hold around her throat released as momentum thrust Metias to one side.

Elena gasped for a full breath. Her legs gave out, and she slid down the wall, desperate for oxygen. A hard thud registered as an eight-year-old hand slid into hers and pulled. She rolled forward onto her knees, trying to get her feet under her, but her body refused to obey her commands.

Metias locked on to her ankle and dragged her back. She was caught between the two of them as the building warned for everyone to get out. Rocketing her free foot back, she slammed her heel into the bastard's face. He let go, and she crawled out of reach.

This was it. This was the moment she left it all behind.

Her mistakes, her failures, the pain of abuse and hunger for something more.

It didn't fit into her life anymore, just as Metias no longer fit. In its place a brightness spread through her where self-punishment had reigned and taken control. A space where possibility and hope flooded through her. One where maybe her and Cash's differences didn't matter. Where they spent mornings curled up in bed, cuddling Bear close as the sun rose over the plateau through the window of his bedroom. She'd pretend to be annoyed at his sarcasm but secretly love it at the same time. He'd send Bear to the kennel and kiss her as though he were starving for her touch. They'd be there for each other when the bad days took over and protect one another from whatever came next. Because that was what two people in love were supposed to do. No games. No manipulation or lies. Pure support and understanding and partnership. It was everything she'd wanted in her marriage and everything she'd been denied by a dominating force she hadn't been strong enough to fight. Until now.

She was going to get out of here. She was going to find him.

Elena tightened her hold on her brother's hand and shoved to her feet. She wanted that life more than anything. The door was right there. She just needed to get to the other side, and they'd be free. She scooped Daniel into her arms, his legs locking around her waist.

A second shot exploded throughout the room.

Elena froze short of the door. She ran her hands the length of Daniel's small rib cage, checking him for wounds, but there was no blood.

Then the pain hit. It stole the air from her lungs and suctioned every thought from her brain.

She'd been checking the wrong body.

In an instant, the life she'd laid out ahead of herself vanished. Her hold on Daniel slipped, and he clutched on so tight she thought the medical examiner who performed her autopsy might see the hand-shaped bruises. He was dragging her down. She dropped to her knees as the tears burned, mixing with the sprinkler water across her face.

"I thought I made myself clear, *mi esposa*." Metias's voice sounded too close yet far away at the same time. "You're not walking away from me again."

"Get up, Lena." Daniel was standing in front of her now. Terrified and desperate with a sob contorting his small face. He pulled on her shirt twice. Three times. Each exposing his lack of strength and helplessness. And her heart broke for him. His life hadn't been nearly long enough. "Come on!"

"Go." Elena shoved at him, tried to put some distance between them as the gut-wrenching throb in her lower back intensified. To give him a chance of survival. But he wouldn't budge. Sweat built along the back of her neck as the reality of their situation set in. She was going to lose him again. No one was coming to save them this time. But she'd fight until her last breath to give him a chance. "It's okay. I'll be fine." She nodded for the door. "I'll find you. Go. Now."

She pried his grip from her shirt. It was going to be okay. One way or another. He'd never have to worry about Metias or the cartel again. Her hand shook as Daniel pulled free. He charged for the door. Pressure increased between her shoulder blades as her ex crossed the room toward her.

"He's never going to make it, Elena. You know that." Deep pain rippled down her back as Metias secured his hand around the tendons in her neck, but it didn't have the power over her he thought it did. "When I'm finished with you, I'm going to find him. I'm going to end your entire family for what you've done."

"That's going to be hard to do." Elena swallowed the pain flaring up her back and down one leg from the bullet still lodged deep in her flesh. She gripped the hammer Daniel had dropped, a leftover tool from the construction on the building, beneath her. "When you're dead."

She rolled onto her side, bringing the iron mallet in contact with the side of Metias's head. Right where he'd struck her with his weapon. He fell back with a groan and landed on top of her outstretched legs. She watched as Daniel wrenched the door open to escape, relief bursting through her chest at the sight.

Only to see him come to a stop as he took in the mountain of muscle and hostility waiting for him on the other side.

CASH GRABBED FOR the boy and hauled Daniel behind him.

The explosion had started a fire on the other side of the building. The flames had reached the hallway and were closing in fast. They didn't have long to get free of the building.

Cash launched at the son of a bitch trying to

get his bearings behind Elena. "Get Daniel out of here! Go!"

He blindsided Metias the moment the cartel lieutenant tried to bring his weapon around.

They collided into the wall on the other side of the room. Cash brought his elbow down into Metias's face while a solid fist to his side knocked the oxygen from his chest. Elena tried to get to all fours in his peripheral vision, but she wasn't making progress. He caught a right hook in the face, twisting him around, but he stopped the second from landing. He pinned Metias against the wall by the throat. "What did you do to her?"

"What I promised." A bloody smile split the lieutenant's mouth at one corner. "You think I would let her walk away from me to be with somebody else? Elena is mine, Mr. Meyers. Till death do us part."

"Do you think this is some kind of duel, you son of a bitch? That whoever is still standing at the end wins the damsel's heart? You're so hard up for attention, you have to threaten, abduct and abuse a woman and her eight-year-old brother to make yourself feel like a man? Well, the world I fight for doesn't work that way. Elena isn't yours. And she isn't mine. She's whoever the hell she wants to be, and neither of us get to say what that is. You're nothing but a dominating and manipulative piece of garbage who gets off on the misery of others." Cash rammed his forehead into the man's face. "And you don't deserve her."

Metias recovered quickly. His backhand connected with the laceration in Cash's temple. The lieutenant followed it up with a two-strike boxer combination. Cash fell back into a table shoved against one wall. Swiping his nose with the back of his hand, he gauged Metias's next move. His ribs protested the twist of his torso and reminded him he was no spring chicken in this fight. He shoved away from the table and hauled his knee into the lieutenant's gut. The cartel leader doubled over, and Cash took advantage. Metias hit the wet carpet, eyes closed against the onslaught of pain and sprinkler water from overhead.

A juvenile scream pierced Cash's eardrums.

He turned to catch a lick of flame crossing the threshold into the room. The sprinklers weren't enough to douse the flames. Daniel had backed himself into the opposite corner, his hands over his ears as he tucked into a ball. Cash lunged for Elena, who lay motionless on the floor. A dark stain spread across her low back. Hell. She'd been shot. Single bullet. No exit wound from what he could tell. "Elle, can you hear me? Come on. Wake up."

No answer.

He had mere minutes to get them out of here. Cash searched for something—anything—to staunch the flow of blood, but the room had been emptied long before he'd found Elena and Daniel inside.

Movement registered in his peripheral vision a split second before a fist jabbed into his ribs. Cash's roar drowned out that of the flames as they flickered through the doorway. Undeniable pain lashed through him. His face hit the floor, fingers biting into the carpet.

A rumble shifted through the room. The building would collapse in on itself at any moment. He had to end this. Now. It was the only way to get Elena and Daniel out of here alive. Cash buried the agony ripping him apart from the inside and shoved upright. The lieutenant came at him again, his arm cocked back.

Metias's knuckles skimmed his ear as Cash dodged the attack. The lieutenant clamped a hand over the bullet wound in Cash's shoulder. The world—the fire, the sprinkler water, the sobs coming from the kid in the corner, even the cartel leader lunging for the gun on the floor—it all sped up as though this were some kind of out-of-body experience. His heart thundered behind his ears as he grabbed Metias's white suit jacket and launched his fist into the bastard's face. Once. Twice. A third time. "You think because you have a minuscule amount of power that you get to hold on to it forever?"

The man's head snapped back on his neck as blood exploded from his nose and mouth. It took everything Cash had to hold the lieutenant upright.

"Cash." That voice. He knew that voice. It'd become part of him the past few days. It'd replaced the inner critic screaming at him that he should've been better, that he should've done better for Wade, that it'd been his fault Alpine Valley had suffered as much as it had. That voice had opened him up to the idea of allowing love and life back in and moving on from the mistakes he'd made in the past.

His vision blurred as he struggled to put Elena in his sights. Whether from the concussion from a day ago or losing too much blood, he didn't know. Metias hung, beaten and weak, in his grip, but right then it didn't matter. Dismantling *Sangre por Sangre* for the sins of his brother didn't matter. Punishing Metias for what he'd done didn't matter.

Elena. Daniel. Getting them free of the violence and trauma they'd suffered at the hands of entitled jerks. That was all he could do. He hadn't been able to save his brother, but he'd be damned if he let the cartel take them. Cash released his hold on the lieutenant and let the bastard hit the floor under his own weight.

"Do it." Metias rolled his head back and forth against the sopping industrial carpet. Blood leaked down his face and stained that once-pristine white suit jacket. "Finish it. If you don't, the people I work for… They will."

The gun was right there. All he had to do was pick it up and seal the lieutenant's fate. Secure Elena's and Daniel's and Alpine Valley's futures. One pull of the trigger. That was all it would take. But Cash wasn't that man, despite his fears that something waited inside of him to claw free as it had spawned from his brother. He didn't get to decide who lived and who died, who he helped and who he punished. And he didn't want that responsibility.

Metias slipped into unconsciousness.

Smoke burned Cash's nostrils. He turned to find tendrils of flames traveling across the ceiling. "The fire will do it for me."

He left Metias there to save himself, extending both hands out for the eight-year-old who'd seen enough nightmares to last him a lifetime. Daniel hesitated, his gaze cutting to his sister and back. "Hi, buddy. I'm Cash. I'm a friend of your sister's. Let's get you back home. Okay?"

The small, rounded face with the same-shaped nose and brown eyes as Elena nodded, then Daniel opened his arms to let Cash pick him up. It took more energy than it should have to lift the kid into his chest, but he wasn't going to let something as minor as a bullet wound and a couple broken ribs stop him from keeping his promise.

"All right. Let's get your sister." Fire trailed up the walls and soon engulfed the entire corner Daniel had huddled against. Cash bit back the moan working up his throat as he crouched to pull Elena into his side. She was conscious—barely—and able to shuffle one foot in front of the other, but it would take all of them working together to escape.

Flames lashed out from the partially finished

walls along the hallway. Cinder blocks hissed as Cash dragged them inch by inch down the corridor. But it wasn't enough. He wasn't enough.

His leg had gone numb. Nothing but a tingling where feeling should be. Blood soaked through the gauze Jocelyn had used to patch the hole in his shoulder. Soon he'd have nothing left but the oxygen in his lungs, and the fire would take care of that in time. His body would shut down until all he was capable of was losing the woman he loved. "We're going to make it."

Every muscle in his body screamed for relief. One more step. Then another. The fire was stretching across the floor, cutting off their escape. Black smoke built along the ceiling, and before he had a chance to warn either Elena or Daniel, they were surrounded. Blind. With no way out.

Coughs seized each of their lungs and seared the back of his throat. He was losing his grip on Daniel despite the lock the kid had around his neck.

"Cash." Elena struggled to stay upright on her own, but Cash wouldn't let go. He couldn't lose her. "It's too late. We'll be trapped. Go. Get Daniel out of here."

"There's no way in hell I'm leaving you." He hauled her into his side. His ribs took the brunt of the impact, but he didn't care. "No matter what happens, we do it together. Got it? You and me and Daniel."

She fisted her hand in his T-shirt.

Cash forced himself to take another step forward. The building groaned as the fire spread. Daniel's cries ricocheted through him. A growl clawed its way up his throat as they moved as one, but the flames were getting too close. "We're going to make it."

There was no other option. The hollowness that'd gutted him over the past year had finally started shrinking. Healing. Because of Elena, and he needed more time. They needed more time.

The alarm cut out. Pops and whistles of the fire closed in from every direction. And in the distance... Barking.

Cash wouldn't let himself latch on to the sound. Because if he did, if he lost his focus for a fraction of a second, Elena and Daniel would pay the price. The barking came again. Closer. Louder. Impossible. "Bear?"

His Rottweiler dove through the flames and landed a few feet in front of him. She hiked onto her back legs in excitement. A wrap of white bandages encircled her midsection, a guiding flag as the smoke thickened. She barked louder than ever before.

"Over here!" a female voice called.

A burst of frigid white clouds fought back the flames enough for him to identify Jocelyn Carville and Jones Driscoll in the corridor. Followed by Scarlett Beam and Granger Morais. The logistics coordinator left the others to continue work on clearing a path while she swung a portable oxygen tank complete with a mask from her back to her front. She closed the distance between them and set the mask over Daniel's mouth and nose. "We're here, Cash. Tell me what you need."

Chapter Fifteen

She wasn't very good at dying. Despite Metias's efforts.

Dim lighting eased through her eyelids. The rhythmic ping of the machine monitoring her heart rate and other stats had been set on low, and there was still an ache in her lower back.

"Welcome back to the land of the living." The voice Elena had feared that first time she'd woken up in this room flooded through her.

Only this time she didn't want to run.

Not that she could with a fresh bullet wound in one of her oblique muscles. She'd been lucky. Another inch to the left, and her ex-husband would've paralyzed or killed her as he'd intended. Her heart hurt at the idea. They'd been happy once, hadn't they? How had it ended like this in such a short amount of time? The questions would always be there. One thing she knew for certain was that no matter what she'd done differently, their story would've ended the same.

Elena tried to sit up higher, but an added weight

prevented her from adjusting. A headful of tussled brown hair tickled the inside skin of her arm, its pint-size owner passed out and tucked into her side. Her legs had gone to sleep from her brother's position over the top of them, but she didn't care. He was alive. He was safe. He was home. Because of Cash.

She swiped the painkiller-induced drowsiness from her eyes, caught off guard by a yawn. She'd let Daniel sleep awhile longer. After everything he'd been through, she didn't see a reason to rush him back to normal. They'd need time, recovery. Together. "Not sure I want to stick around. Getting shot hurts."

The world had gone on living, but so much had changed.

Cash's low laugh filled the room with a warmth she'd missed. His upper body was stiff with the sling supporting his left arm and shoulder. He leaned forward in the chair, pulling a package from behind him with his uninjured hand. Gift wrapped with a bow. "You might change your mind after you see what Bear got for you. She felt bad about before. Thought she could make it up to you."

Setting it on her lap, he took a seat on the edge of the bed, those compelling dark eyes sliding to Daniel to ensure he hadn't jostled her brother awake. It was the little considerations like that—awareness of the people and their needs around him—that she loved the most.

There was that word again. Love. She thought

she'd been in love once before. She'd been willing to follow it through countless lies, secrecy and abusive behavior. Only to end up running from it altogether.

This…felt different. Whole. As though she'd been missing a piece of herself all her life, and no matter how many times she'd tried to fill that hole, the puzzle pieces didn't fit. Until now. Because the missing piece wasn't escaping Metias, wasn't bringing her brother home or falling for Cash. It was learning to trust again. Having the courage to stand up for others. And forgiving those who'd wished her dead, including Deputy McCrae and her ex. All of it countered the pain and betrayal she'd suffered at the hands of others and gave her the greatest gift she could imagine. Love for herself. And for the man who'd charged into her life with a gun in one hand and an offer of survival in the other.

"Bear is an excellent gift wrapper." Elena pulled at the jute string expertly tied around the package and let the fabric fall away. Bright blue packaging peeked out from inside. "You brought me Oreos." Her stomach lurched at the memory of the last time she'd taken a bite out of one of Cash's cookies. "I'm not going to throw up after I eat them, right?"

"Depends on how many you eat in one sitting, but no." He grabbed for the package's tab and pulled as slowly as possible to keep the noise down. Daniel stirred but refused to wake. She knew that a bomb could go off in this room and the eight-year-old wouldn't notice. But she appreciated Cash's effort all the same. "They're not laced with dog medication, if that's what you're getting at. It's a brand-new package."

"Thank you." She pried a single cookie from the sleeve and took a bite, watching him do the same. Double-stuffed. Even better. The sugar hit her system almost instantly, but her stomach wasn't quite convinced it was safe. Well worth any nausea. "For everything. Daniel and I wouldn't be here if it weren't for you."

"From what I saw when I walked in that room, Metias was the one in trouble. I could see it in your eyes. You weren't going to let him push you around anymore," he said. "I was just there for support."

She raised her hand then, tentative and slow, as though approaching a wild animal. Tracing his bottom lip, she avoided the cut matching hers. There were others. At his temple, across his knuckles, along his handsome face. Every one of them had been earned from his choice to protect and fight for her. "Support looks good on you."

Her gaze drifted to the bullet wound in his shoulder, to the gauze taped beneath his shirt, and remembered what had led to him getting shot in the first place. Deputy McCrae's words were there, right at the front of her mind, and wouldn't let up. But she didn't want to lose this feeling. She didn't want to go back to being unable to trust him or wondering if he was hiding something from her. She'd had an entire marriage made of lies. She couldn't do that again.

"Ask me. You have the right to know." He'd read her mind again. She didn't have any explanation for it other than the fact that when two people survived what they had together, when they fought side by side for one another, they were exposed and vulnerable to that person. Cash slid off the edge of the bed, and those mere inches of distance between them stabbed through her. "Ask me."

"Is it true? What McCrae said at the station? Were you the one who was supposed to warn us the cartel was coming?" Her voice didn't sound like her own, but rather a puppeteer using her.

"Yes." He stared down at her, all heat and sorrow and stillness. "I was a forward observer in the Marine Corps. It was my job to see the threat coming before it struck. I studied patterns of attacks and consulted my commanding officers on how to respond or which targets to strategize around."

"And you do the same job for Socorro." It wasn't a question. McCrae had made it clear when he'd laid the cartel's sins at Cash's feet at the station. Though at the time, she hadn't put much stock in his words while he was holding a gun to her head. A tear escaped down her face without her intention, and she wiped it away with the back of her hand. "So what happened the night of the raid? Why didn't you warn us before *Sangre por Sangre* attacked?"

"Wade happened," he said.

That name—so simple and yet so heavy—pressurized air in her chest. The monitor to the side of her bed responded with an uptick of her heart rate for all to hear. Cash wasn't the type of operator to let his personal issues interfere with his work. He was one of the most focused and determined men she'd ever met. So if a dead man's history had somehow interfered with Cash's job, there was only one explanation as to why. Her voice broke. "You found him."

"Yeah." Cash lowered his voice, as though not quite able to wrap his head around his own words. "I found him."

"When you said his tattoo was how you and Bear identified him, you meant that night of the raid. You've been looking for him all this time." Elena grabbed his uninjured hand in both of hers. The wound in her back hollered for her attention, and she had to right herself to get it to stop.

Concern deepened the lines between his brows, and Cash dropped to his knees. He took her hand in his, letting her squeeze out her pain. "Take it easy. I'm here."

Her fingers brushed through Daniel's hair as she breathed through the upset in her back. She didn't know what she would've done had her brother not come home. Elena memorized the shape of his face, how his nose turned up at the end, and it was easy to imagine him asleep right there in her lap as something more permanent.

She knew what she would've done.

She wouldn't have ever stopped. The cartel would've had to kill her before she accepted defeat. She would've done whatever it took to hold him again. She'd broken into a cartel compound. She'd partnered with military contractors. She'd faced her worst nightmare. All for the chance of accomplishing what Cash had. And blaming him for letting his heart lead him that night instead of his head didn't feel right. "I'm so sorry."

"No. I am." He skimmed a calloused thumb under her eye and caught a wayward tear before it fell. "I should've told you the truth from the beginning, but I was scared if I did, you'd see me as someone just like the people we were fighting. That you wouldn't want me. I've spent years surrounded by a team I trust, but I'd never felt so alone as I did when Wade died. Then you came along. You're the most incredible woman I've ever met. You're stronger than I am, more courageous. You'll fight until your last breath for the people you love, and I wanted to be one of those people, Elena. Because I love you."

"How could I not want someone as inspiring and humane and hopeful as you are?" Her smile tugged at the laceration in her bottom lip. "If I'm any of those things you just said, it's because you were the one to show me how first. You're everything I've been missing, Cash. I love you, too."

He lunged from his kneeled position on the floor and crushed his mouth to hers. The impact pushed her deeper into the bed, but Elena found herself wanting him even closer. Bullet wounds be damned. She dragged him over the edge of the bed, and the monitor off to the side spiked with an erratic beat.

"What are you guys doing?" a small voice asked.

She broke the kiss, letting her breath come back to her. Heat flooded her face and neck. Her brother had just witnessed her making out with a man in the middle of a hospital room.

"Hey, buddy. Remember me?" Cash offered one hand in greeting. "I'm Cash."

FIRE AND RESCUE never recovered Metias's body from the compound.

Midday sun beat down on the back of his neck as Cash straightened. He chugged a mouthful of water as he took in the dozens of helping hands working to rebuild Alpine Valley.

It wasn't hard to imagine the cartel lieutenant had run with his tail between his legs. No purchases on his debit or credit cards. No cell usage or hits on any of the aliases Elena had catalogued over the course of her marriage to the son of a bitch. Even the Albuquerque house had been emptied. From what Cash knew of *Sangre por Sangre* upper management, Metias was living on borrowed time. What he'd done in the cartel's name was bad for business. And they wouldn't let that slide.

The DEA had rounded up a handful of soldiers and seized multiple shipments of drugs. The kids Metias had abducted and started training were left to social services, which was in the process of identifying and hunting down their families. Though some had been with the cartel for so long, they weren't quite sure where they belonged.

That was where Elena came in.

She searched missing person reports, local interviews and witness statements, and she administered and collected DNA tests from those kids the cartel had abandoned after the fire. She was doing everything in her power to ensure each of them made it back home to their families, and she hadn't stopped since the moment Doc Piel had cleared her to leave the medical suite. The woman was unlike anything he'd encountered, even in war-torn cities and towns overseas. She cared truly and deeply about every kid she was helping, and he loved her for it.

A loud bark sounded from the ground, and he caught sight of Bear directly under his position. She was signaling the approaching SUV as though she'd sensed them from a mile away. Which was entirely possible considering who was rolling up on the construction site.

Cash holstered the hammer in his work belt and made his way toward the ladder braced against the framing he and a few other locals had put together over the past couple of days. Fixing what the cartel had destroyed was slow but rewarding. Clearing the debris, replacing broken windows, sanding down and painting singed siding, patching bullet holes in the stucco—it all served to ease the weight he'd carried these past couple weeks. But it was rebuilding the family home that'd served as a refuge for Elena that bridged the grief between who he'd been and who he wanted to be for her.

The SUV pulled to a stop along the curb just as Cash's boots touched down on solid earth. Jocelyn and Maverick rounded the head of the vehicle. She brought her hand up to block the sun from her eyes. "It's looking good considering there was nothing here but a pile of ashes a week ago."

"It's coming along." He wiped his sweaty hands on a towel hanging off his belt. "She hasn't seen it yet. I was kind of hoping it'd be a surprise, but it's getting harder to keep her away every day. It's only a matter of time before she finds me out." Cash tried to read the logistics operator's motive for coming into town. "You here to bring me lunch or what?"

Maverick bolted straight for Bear, and the two started chasing each other around the worksite. Her ribs were on the mend, and if Metias hadn't shot the man responsible for kicking Cash's dog in the side, Cash would've returned the favor the first chance he'd gotten.

News of Deputy McCrae's actions had spread like wildfire, and the people of this town were ticked off. With reason. State police were now investigating McCrae's reach and misconduct while also vetting every other officer in the department. Some hadn't passed with flying colors, but there were no signs the chief of police had anything to do with what'd gone down. That left Alpine Valley more shorthanded than they'd already been, but sometimes the smallest forces made the biggest impact.

"I brought you something else." There was a heaviness to Jocelyn's voice he didn't like. Someone who baked cookies and hosted Christmas parties shouldn't sound like she did. She pulled a set of photos from a file folder she'd tucked under her arm. "Looks like Elena won't have to file those divorce papers after all."

Hell. Cash shuffled through the photos, each one more detailed than the last. Remnants of a white suit stood out in one. "Metias?"

"We found him about two miles east of Albuquerque. Took some doing," Jocelyn said. "They tried to hide their work, but a hitchhiker had seen the smoke and went to investigate for herself."

It was a common punishment among cartel families. A warning. The tire strung around the victim's neck would have been filled with an accelerant—most likely gasoline. Untraceable and cheap. Once the fire had been extinguished, there would've been little trace of the body or those responsible. "DNA?"

"They're working on it. Teeth were busted. They worked him over at least a couple hours before they put him out of his misery, but the ME is hoping there's something salvageable from bone marrow for a comparison and ID." Jocelyn's voice softened. "You want me to tell her?"

"No. I'm heading to meet up with her in a few minutes." Cash handed back the photos. He wouldn't need them. "I'll tell her. Thanks anyway. You coming to the service?"

"I'll be there." Jocelyn took a couple steps back. "Just got to run these by the police chief first."

He whistled to get Bear's attention, and both Maverick and she responded by returning to their handler's sides. In less than a minute, Jocelyn was behind the wheel of her SUV, pulling away from the curb. Cash scratched behind Bear's ear as he watched them go. "Let's go see Mama."

The Rottweiler's tail double-timed it at the mention of Elena's new nickname all the way to the truck. Cash tossed in his work belt, calling his goodbye over the bed to the men and women continuing work on the house. Pulling a flannel shirt from the back seat, he picked off clots of dog hair and threaded his arms into both sides. Not exactly appropriate attire for a funeral, but he wasn't a suit kind of guy. Never had been.

He hauled himself into the driver's seat. His shoulder pinched at the motion, but the more he put it to work, the better it felt. That was the thing about taking a bullet. You either came back stronger or you let it put you out of the game for good. And he wasn't finished.

Trees blurred through the side windows as he wound his way through town. He'd been all over the world during three tours in the Corps, but nowhere felt like Alpine Valley did. Like home. Cash pulled onto a single lane stretch of asphalt that was fenced off with overgrown trees and over two acres of headstones. And right there at the gate was the reason he had no interest in ever leaving this place.

Bear huffed to be let out of the truck the moment she saw Elena, and Cash understood that more than most. Just being near that woman was special. They both felt it. "Yeah, yeah. I'm moving. Hold your horses, dog."

He shoved out of the truck, nearly getting run over by Bear's insistence to reach Elena first. A wide smile transformed the woman's face as the Rottweiler bounded straight for her. Bear was practically climbing up Elena by the time he reached her, and Cash dragged the dog back. "Hey, no jumping." Every cell in his body was pulled in by hers, and Cash leaned in to show her exactly how much he'd missed her most of the day. "Hi."

"Hi. You must be working hard over there at the site." She leaned into her crutch, staring up at him as though he were the most important person in the world. And, hell, if he didn't want to be that for her. Her support system, her protector, her hero. Because she deserved it all. "I haven't seen you all day. How's the rebuild coming along?"

"Great. Moving faster than we expected, but it's hard to slow down with so many helping hands." Cash took her crutch for her, letting her use him any way she needed. The armrest tended to chafe with how much she was on her feet collecting information on the kids from the compound. If it was up to him, he'd be there with her all day. But kids who'd been taken from their homes, from their families, didn't trust men like him. Soldiers. Strangers. They only trusted Elena, and he didn't blame them a bit. "Jocelyn visited the site a little while ago. Wanted to let you know they found Metias."

"Oh?" she asked. "What hole he did crawl inside?"

"He didn't, Elena." Cash kept his hand on her elbow in case the news hit harder than he expected. "They found him. With a tire around his neck."

"The cartel killed him." She didn't let her emotions betray her. It was a habit she'd had to learn during her marriage to Metias, but he hoped, with time, she'd realize she didn't ever have to hide from him.

"I'm sorry." He didn't really know if that was true after what they'd been through.

"Me, too. But it's over now, isn't it? We don't have to spend the rest of our lives looking over our shoulders. Wondering if he'll come back." Elena's hand on his arm was grounding and exciting all at the same time. A single touch was all he needed, and everything outside the bubble they built around themselves didn't seem so important. "Are you ready for this? We don't have to go in. We can send everyone home, go back to Socorro, stay in the room and forget the world exists."

"I'm good." And he meant it. From the ashes of grief, loss, fear and betrayal, something new had been born inside of him. Becoming a private military contractor had given him a sense of purpose after Wade's death, but it was this new life he and Elena were in the process of building for themselves that kept him going. "I've been waiting for this day for a long time."

They walked through the cemetery's gates as one and headed for the small gathering of people waiting beside the casket. They all looked up at him as they approached and cleared a path to give him and Elena a front-row seat. Seven in total, including Elena's parents. The headstone had already been installed.

Wade Meyers. Beloved son, brother and friend.

The bishop of the local church greeted the attendees and asked if there was anyone who'd like to say something about the deceased, but Cash only had attention for the way Bear sat at the head of the gleaming wood of the casket. Her eyes had started watering as though she knew exactly who was inside that box. The rest of the Socorro team had noticed, too. There would be no military funeral. No seven-gun salute or hammering of pins into the wood. All eyes were on her, and no eulogy would meet the hurt Bear felt from losing her best friend. And it was enough.

"Rest in peace, brother." Cash unpocketed the medal he'd been given the day he and Wade had enlisted in the military. His father's. It was his brother's turn to hang on to it now. He set it on top of the wood and watched as the casket was lowered into the ground. Within minutes, the service was over. Condolences and handshakes passed in a blur, and soon, he and Elena and Bear were the only ones left at the grave site.

"Tell me what you're thinking," she said.

"I'm thinking it's time to go home and appreciate the life I have left. With you, Bear and your family." Cash took her hand in his and planted a kiss on her mouth. She tasted just as he remembered. Of hope. Of love. And a little bit of Oreo frosting. "What do you say?"

"I'll go home with you on one condition—" Elena

flashed a wide smile up at him "—Bear spends tonight in the kennel."

Cash wrapped his arms around her midback and kissed her again. "I think that can be arranged."

* * * * *

#2199 A PLACE TO HIDE
Lookout Mountain Mysteries • by Debra Webb
Two and a half years ago, Grace Myers, infant son in tow, escaped a serial killer. Now, she'll have to trust Deputy Robert Vaughn to safeguard their identities and lives. The culprit is still on the loose and determined to get even...

#2200 WETLANDS INVESTIGATION
The Swamp Slayings • by Carla Cassidy
Investigator Nick Cain is in the small town of Black Bayou for one reason—to catch a serial killer. But between his unwanted attraction to his partner Officer Sarah Beauregard and all the deadly town secrets he uncovers, will his plan to catch the killer implode?

#2201 K-9 DETECTION
New Mexico Guard Dogs • by Nichole Severn
Jocelyn Carville knows a dangerous cartel is responsible for the Alpine Valley PD station bombing. But convincing Captain Baker Halsey is harder than uncovering the cartel's motive. Until the syndicate's next attack makes their risky partnership inevitable...

#2202 SWIFTWATER ENEMIES
Big Sky Search and Rescue • by Danica Winters
When Aspen Stevens and Detective Leo West meet at a crime scene, they instantly dislike each other. But uncovering the truth about their victim means combining search and rescue expertise and acknowledging the fine line between love and hate even as they risk their lives...

#2203 THE PERFECT WITNESS
Secure One • by Katie Mettner
Security expert Cal Newfellow knows safety is an illusion. But when he's tasked with protecting Marlise, a prosecutor's star witness against an infamous trafficker and murderer, he'll do everything in his power to keep the danger—and his heart—away from her.

#2204 MURDER IN THE BLUE RIDGE MOUNTAINS
The Lynleys of Law Enforcement • by R. Barri Flowers
After a body is discovered in the mountains, special agent Garrett Sneed returns home to work the case with his ex, law enforcement ranger Madison Lynley. Before long, their attraction is heating up...until another homicide reveals a possible link to his mother's unsolved murder. And then the killer sets his sights on Madison...

Get 3 FREE REWARDS!

We'll send you 2 FREE Books plus a FREE Mystery Gift.

FREE
Value Over
$20

Both the **Harlequin Intrigue**® and **Harlequin**® Romantic Suspense series feature compelling novels filled with heart-racing action-packed romance that will keep you on the edge of your seat.

YES! Please send me 2 FREE novels from the Harlequin Intrigue or Harlequin Romantic Suspense series and my FREE gift (gift is worth about $10 retail). After receiving them, if I don't wish to receive any more books, I can return the shipping statement marked "cancel." If I don't cancel, I will receive 6 brand-new Harlequin Intrigue Larger-Print books every month and be billed just $6.49 each in the U.S. or $6.99 each in Canada, a savings of at least 13% off the cover price, or 4 brand-new Harlequin Romantic Suspense books every month and be billed just $5.49 each in the U.S. or $6.24 each in Canada, a savings of at least 12% off the cover price. It's quite a bargain! Shipping and handling is just 50¢ per book in the U.S. and $1.25 per book in Canada.* I understand that accepting the 2 free books and gift places me under no obligation to buy anything. I can always return a shipment and cancel at any time by calling the number below. The free books and gift are mine to keep no matter what I decide.

Choose one: ☐ **Harlequin Intrigue Larger-Print** (199/399 BPA GRMX)   ☐ **Harlequin Romantic Suspense** (240/340 BPA GRMX)   ☐ **Or Try Both!** (199/399 & 240/340 BPA GRQD)

Name (please print)

Address   Apt. #

City   State/Province   Zip/Postal Code

Email: Please check this box ☐ if you would like to receive newsletters and promotional emails from Harlequin Enterprises ULC and its affiliates. You can unsubscribe anytime.

Mail to the **Harlequin Reader Service:**
IN U.S.A.: P.O. Box 1341, Buffalo, NY 14240-8531
IN CANADA: P.O. Box 603, Fort Erie, Ontario L2A 5X3

Want to try 2 free books from another series? Call 1-800-873-8635 or visit www.ReaderService.com.

*Terms and prices subject to change without notice. Prices do not include sales taxes, which will be charged (if applicable) based on your state or country of residence. Canadian residents will be charged applicable taxes. Offer not valid in Quebec. This offer is limited to one order per household. Books received may not be as shown. Not valid for current subscribers to the Harlequin Intrigue or Harlequin Romantic Suspense series. All orders subject to approval. Credit or debit balances in a customer's account(s) may be offset by any other outstanding balance owed by or to the customer. Please allow 4 to 6 weeks for delivery. Offer available while quantities last.

Your Privacy—Your information is being collected by Harlequin Enterprises ULC, operating as Harlequin Reader Service. For a complete summary of the information we collect, how we use this information and to whom it is disclosed, please visit our privacy notice located at corporate.harlequin.com/privacy-notice. From time to time we may also exchange your personal information with reputable third parties. If you wish to opt out of this sharing of your personal information, please visit readerservice.com/consumerschoice or call 1-800-873-8635. **Notice to California Residents**—Under California law, you have specific rights to control and access your data. For more information on these rights and how to exercise them, visit corporate.harlequin.com/california-privacy.

HIHRS23